The Forgotten History of India

The Forgotten History of India

Arun Anand

Published by
PRABHAT PRAKASHAN PVT. LTD.
4/19 Asaf Ali Road,
New Delhi-110 002 (INDIA)
e-mail: prabhatbooks@gmail.com

ISBN 978-93-5521-186-6
THE FORGOTTEN HISTORY OF INDIA
by Shri Arun Anand

Edition
2026

Paperback Price
₹ 400.00 (Rupees Four Hundred only)

Printed at
R-Tech Offset Printers, Delhi

For Tejas

Preface

This book has taken shape over the last five-years as I researched on various subjects for my columns. This research introduced me to several forgotten chapters of Indian history. I came across several startling facts and realised there were many unsung heroes as well as the dark and the glorious chapters of Indian history that haven't been told to us.

This forgotten history of India needs to be told as it might help us to understand the fault lines created deliberately within Indian society by propagating myths as facts and facts as fallacies.

The way we have been taught 'history' in schools and universities make it difficult to fathom that 'history' can be an interesting subject also and we must know our real history. I have deliberately kept every chapter short so that the readers do not lose interest while reading. Hence, in every chapter, I have tried to tell a story and used anecdotes to make the reading interesting and relevant.

In this journey, I came across several untapped

primary and secondary sources of information which throw a new light on developments that have shaped India's public discourse over the last seven and a half decades. These sources are mentioned in various chapters. Hopefully, this would help the readers who want to delve deeper into areas of their interest.

A substantial part of the book deals with myths and propaganda related to Rashtriya Swayamsevak Sangh(RSS) as the history of India especially in the post-independence era is entwined to the evolution of the RSS. I have tried to take a closer look at some of the 'stereotypes' created about RSS as to how close they are to reality. The readers are free to draw their conclusions as I haven't presented an opinion but tried to share the facts, figures and the historical evidence backed by authentic references.

I want to thank my friends, associates, and editors from all those media organisations for whom I wrote over the last many years.

Most importantly, I want to thank my readers who take out time, spend their hard-earned money to buy my books and graciously share their feedback. Your feedback for this book is also much awaited.

—Arun Anand

Contents

1

Nehru vs Organiser: Battle that Led to Restrictions on Freedom of Expression

Even as the debate over the freedom of expression and speech in India has been continuing for decades with questions being raised about applicability of sedition laws especially in case of media and journalists, the irony of the situation can't be lost as those who curbed the freedom of expression are questioning the curbs!

Around six decades ago, the first amendment to the Constitution of India was brought by Congress government led by Jawaharlal Nehru. This amendment, in addition to bringing sweeping changes in laws related to socio-economic issues, also drastically curbed the freedom of speech.

It was an outcome of the Nehru government's intent to clamp down on voices critical of the government. Incidentally, one of the immediate triggers for restricting freedom of expression by Nehru was primarily the battle between him and

Organiser, an English weekly backed by the Rashtriya Swayamsevak Sangh (RSS).

Organiser vs Nehru

Organiser was quite critical of the Nehru government in the wake of the partition of India in 1947 and widespread communal violence against Hindus in Dhaka and several other parts of Pakistan. In February, 1950, the weekly published several reports critical of the Nehru government. These reports criticised Nehru's policies and brought to the fore the plight of thousands of Hindu refugees who were forced to migrate from East Pakistan to West Bengal after they were targeted in widespread communal violence. The weekly demanded that the Muslim evacuee property should be distributed to Hindu refugees as they were forced to exchange blood for bread at blood banks.

As Nehru was facing heavy criticism for proposing confidence-building measures with Pakistan's Prime Minister Liaquat Ali Khan while Hindus were being targeted, the weekly published cartoons of Nehru and Liaquat and in a piece titled 'Villains vs Fools', it wrote, "The villainy of Pakistan can be matched only by our own idiocy."

An infuriated Nehru decided to clamp down on Organiser. On 2 March, 1950, the Central Press Advisory Committee, a regulatory body under the Nehru government met to discuss what had been published by the weekly. On the same day itself, an order to gag the weekly was issued by the Chief Commissioner of

Delhi. It was a 'pre-censorship order' and was issued under the notorious East Punjab Public Safety Act. This order made it mandatory for the editor and the publisher to submit to the government for approval all content related to communal issues or Pakistan. It also included cartoons!

KR Malkani, the editor of Organiser was not to be cowed down. Malkani, who later became a Bhartiya Jana Sangh (BJS) and Bharatiya Janata Party (BJP) stalwart, hit back at this gagging order with a bold editorial on 13 March: "If the administration earnestly wants ugly facts not to appear in the press, the only right and honest course for it is effectively to exert itself for the non-occurence of such brutal facts. Suppression of facts is no solution to the Bengal tragedy. Surely the government does not hope to extinguish a volcano by squatting more tightly on its crater."

Battle in the Court

On 10 April, 1950, Organiser's publisher and printer Brij Bhushan and Malkani went to the Supreme Court to get the pre-censorship order quashed. Organiser was represented in the court by NC Chatterjee who was a former president of the Hindu Mahasabha and whose son Somnath Chatterjee later became a Left stalwart. In this famous case which is known in Constitutional history as Brij Bhushan vs The State of Delhi, Chatterjee argued that the pre-censorship order was an infringement on the freedom of speech. He also argued that the law under which this order has been issued doesn't fall under any provisions in the Constitution of India. So the government's pre-censorship order is illegal.

The case got widespread attention and ignited a nationwide debate. The Chief Justice of Bombay High Court, Justice MC Chagla castigated the Nehru government in a public lecture at Poona (now Pune) on 1 May. He said, "The Constitution had not left it to the party in power in the legislature or the caprice of the executive to limit, control or impair any fundamental rights.The right to express opinion, however critical it might be of the government or society as constituted, was one of the most fundamental rights of the individual in a democratic form of government."

PR Das, a prominent jurist, former judge of Patna High Court and brother of Congress stalwart CR Das, remarked, "The danger which I apprehend is that the government may suppress all political parties which do not believe in the Congress government on the plea that the interests of the public order demand that these parties should be suppressed."

Noted jurist and Governor of Bengal at that time Kailash Nath Katju warned, "We must take care that in the name of preservation of state and stopping of subversive activities, we may not stifle democracy itself."

The Verdict

The Supreme Court gave its verdict in this case on 26 May, 1950, in favour of Organiser quashing the pre-censorship order. The Court order said that under

Article 19 of the Constitution, restrictions could be imposed on freedom of expression only in certain cases which were given in clause 2 of the Article. Public order was not one of the grounds so no restriction on the freedom of expression could be imposed on the grounds of 'Public order'.

Following this defeat of his government in the Court against Organiser, Nehru then pushed for introducing more curbs on freedom of expression through the first amendment. Despite fierce resistance from within his party as well as in parliament and media on the issue of freedom of expression, Nehru moved the Constitution (First Amendment) Act, 1951 on 10 May, 1951, and it was enacted by Parliament on 18 June, 1951.

References:

1. 'Sixteen Stormy Days' by Tripurdaman Singh, Penguin Random House India',
2. Archives of Organiser,
3. 'Selected Works of Jawaharlal Nehru' (New Delhi, Jawaharlal Nehru Memorial Fund)

❑

2

How RSS Helped Save 'Darbar Sahib' Twice

The RSS had defended one of the sacred Sikh Shrines the 'Darbar Sahib' at Amritsar twice when Muslim League-led mobs attacked it in 1947. The Sangh came out to protect Sikhs during anti-Sikh riots in 1984. And on 25 June, 1989, 21 RSS swayamsevaks sacrificed their lives against terrorism in Punjab when an RSS Shakha, held in a park, came under a terror attack at Moga. These swayamsevaks were shot dead. An RSS resolution, in the wake of this tragedy, had emphasised about the importance of collective efforts for nation-building.

The connection between the RSS and Sikhs has a historical context. During partition of India in 1947, the RSS saved the lives of a large number Sikhs and played a major role in protecting the population of Punjab from the onslaught of Muslim League-led mobs. It also helped to mobilise them to move to safer places.

The English Tribune wrote during that era, "Punjab is the sword arm of Hindustan and RSS is the sword arm of Punjab". ('The Saffron Surge: Untold Story of RSS Leadership', Prabhat Prakashan)

How Sangh Swayamsevaks fought to protect 'Darbar Sahib'

Manikchandra Vajpayee and Sridhar Paradkar have mentioned in detail these two incidents in their seminal work, 'Partition Days: The Fiery Saga of RSS'. The first attack came on the night of 6 March, 1947. Vajpayee and Paradkar have described: "It was a terrible night of 6 March.A formidable, organised mob of Muslims led by National Guards in their uniform was advancing from Sherawala Gate to Chowk Fawara in Amritsar. This time their target was the well-known Krishna Textile market and sacred Darbar Sahib. But the moment they reached Chowk Fawara, they were fiercely attacked from all sides with lathis, swords, spears, knives and bombs. The mob saw that the attackers were none other but the Knickerwalas (RSS volunteers known as swayamsevaks were identified by their Khaki shorts during that era). They had taken such fright of the swayamsevaks' past record that they ran away. Thus, the victory under the leadership of brave swayamsevaks saved both the Krishna market and Darbar Sahib from destruction."

The RSS posted 75 swayamsevaks (the complete list with names and addresses is available in the appendix of 'Partition Days: The Fiery Saga of RSS') full-time to safeguard the Darbar Sahib from any further onslaught. The RSS' operations to protect the Darbar Sahib were primarily led by Dr Baldev Prakash, the then chief of the RSS' evening shakhas in Amritsar along with the town pracharak (full-time worker) Dr Indrapal and Goverdhan Chopra, in-charge of morning shakhas in Amritsar.

The second attack by Muslim mobs on Darbar Sahib began on 9 March. Vajpayee and Paradkar have given a blow-by-blow account of this incident too.

"That day 9 March, 1947, troops of uniformed Muslim National Guards began to advance towards the Gurudwara from three sides. A big contingent was advancing from the League's stronghold in Katra Karma Singh, the second from Namak Mandi and the third from Sherawala Darwaza. All of them were armed."

"There were a handful of sewadars and they were frightened. Unfortunately, about a hundred unarmed pilgrims were also trapped inside. Because of the curfew they could not leave. Jathas of Sikhs from the rural areas who were coming on receiving information about the situation were stopped outside by armed policemen. This had been done in conspiracy with the League. Phone calls were coming to the Punjab relief committee office from the Gurudwara saying Muslim mobs were advancing towards the Darbar Sahib and the Golden temple was in danger. 'Would you swayamsevaks not come to our aid?' Durga Das Khanna, in-charge of the Karyalaya (RSS office) kept assuring them— 'Do not panic, swayamsevaks have reached there and they have taken up positions in every lane. Whatever the cost we will not let anything happen to the sacred Darbar Sahib. This time to we will teach the Muslims a lesson'."

The Muslim groups were advancing but the swayamsevaks were also alert. Dr Baldev Prakash had also reached there with a team of swayamsevaks. Every mohalla and every house had already turned into a fortress. "This time the plan was not just self-defence but counter attack." The first confrontation was at Chowk Fawara. Muslim mobs had to retreat after some fighting. The mobs had to retreat at other places as well.

"Now the tables were decisively turned. The attackers were on the run and the defenders were chasing them and punishing them. The whole city rang with the shouts of 'Har Har Mahadev' and 'Sat Shri Akaal'."

Prof AN Bali has given a detailed description of how the RSS saved a large number of Sikhs and Hindus in the run-up to the partition. Prof Bali taught in Panjab University and was a resident of Lahore. The book titled 'Now It Can Be Told' was first published in 1949 and the preface was written by Master Tara Singh, a Sikh stalwart who played a key role in shaping up of the Akali movement as well as the emergence of Shiromani Gurdwara Prabhandak Committee as a key body of Sikhs.

Bali, giving a first-hand account of events he witnessed in Lahore, writes, "The police was mostly League minded...who else came to the rescue of the people at this stage but a band of young selfless

Hindus, known as RSS. They organised groups in every mohalla (area) of every town of the province the evacuation of the Hindu and Sikh women and children from dangerous pockets to comparatively safe centres. They arranged for their food, medical aid, clothing and care; even fire brigades were formed in various towns."

"Their (RSS) discipline, their physical fitness and their selflessness in the face of dangers came to the rescue of the people in Punjab when the whole province was burning and when the Congress leaders were helplessly fiddling in New Delhi, not being able to overcome the opposition to the Muslim League and the obstinacy of the governor-general to their proposal for stronger action for the maintenance of law and order."

Noted columnist and author Khushwant Singh had said after the anti-Sikh riots in 1984, "RSS has played an honourable role in maintaining Hindu-Sikh unity before and after the murder of Indira Gandhi in Delhi and in other places. It was the Congress (I) leaders who instigated mobs in 1984 and got more than 3000 people killed. I must give due credit to RSS and the Bharatiya Janata Party (BJP) for showing courage and protecting helpless Sikhs during those difficult days. Atal Bihari Vajpayee himself intervened at a couple of places to help poor taxi drivers."

❑

3

How RSS Played a Key Role in the Liberation of Dadra and Nagar Haveli

The date of 2 August, 1954, is an almost forgotten chapter of Indian history. It centres on Dadra and Nagar Haveli—now a Union territory, the two small enclaves that didn't get independence on 15 August, 1947.

They continued to be ruled by the Portuguese till an armed revolution liberated them, and the Tricolour was unfurled at Silvassa on 2 August, 1954.

The armed revolutionaries then handed these enclaves to the Indian government. However, it took some time before Dadra and Nagar Haveli were formally recognised as an integral part of India, because Portugal had taken the matter to international fora and contested the Indian government's claims.

Unlike what happened during Goa's liberation in 1961, there was no direct intervention by the Indian armed forces in the case of Dadra and Nagar Haveli.

The uprooting of Portuguese rule could be credited largely to armed revolutionaries that included a large number of swayamsevaks (volunteers) of the Rashtriya Swayamsevak Sangh (RSS).

Dadra and Nagar Haveli

The Portuguese had occupied Dadra in 1783, and Nagar Haveli in 1785.

The latter has an area of around 8 square kilometres, and the former of 479 square kilometres. In all, there were 72 villages in these two enclaves, and the population was then around 42,000.

Most of the residents were from the Warlis tribe. After the Portuguese occupied these enclaves, there were several violent clashes with the Raja of Dharampur, who was earlier the ruler of Dadra and Nagar Haveli.

The freedom movement against the Portuguese rule in Goa, which gained momentum in the 1930s, also fuelled the freedom movement in Dadra and Nagar Haveli.

Finally, freedom fighters under the banner of the Azad Gomantak Party and some other organisations unfurled the national flag at Silvassa on 2 August, 1954.

The RSS Role

The official website of the RSS says, "Swayamsevaks liberated the Dadra and Nagar Haveli from Portuguese control on 2 August and handed over the region to central government."

Apart from this, several texts have referred to the RSS' role in the liberation of these enclaves.

The late RSS stalwart, MP and journalist KR Malkani wrote in his book, 'The RSS Story', "On 2 August, 1954, some 200 RSS workers led by Nana Kajrekar and Sudhir Phadke, liberated Dadra and Nagar Haveli, Portuguese enclaves, and put to flight 175 soldiers armed with rifles, Bren guns and Sten guns."

Similar references have been made in 'Sangh and Swaraj' by author Ratan Sharda; 'RSS: A Vision in Action' by former Sangh sarkaryavah HV Seshadri; and 'RSS: Myth and Reality' by the late BJP MP Dinanath Mishra.

Dr Pundalik A Gaitonde, a Goan surgeon and an active participant in the state's liberation movement who was nominated by the President to Parliament in 1962, has discussed in his book 'The Liberation of Goa' how the Azad Gomantak Dal was helped in Dadra and Nagar Haveli by some members of the RSS.

Author Suchitra Kulkarni says in her book 'RSS-BJP Symbiosis: On the Cusp of Culture and Politics', "The RSS played an important role in the liberation of Dadra and Nagar Haveli in 1954-55 and later in 1961, in the liberation of Goa from the Portuguese rule... Several swayamsevaks lost their lives and many were injured in the firings by the Portuguese forces."

According to an August 2011 report in the RSS-backed weekly Organiser, "A function was organised in Pune on 3 August to pay tribute to those RSS freedom fighters who dedicated their lives for the liberation of Dadra and Nagar Haveli from the Portuguese in 1954. Senior historian Shri Babasaheb Purandare addressed the gathering of these freedom fighters which was organised by the Dadra Nagar Haveli Mukti Sangram Samiti.

"One hundred and three members of the Rashtriya Swayamsevak Sangh (RSS) including Shri Purandare had forced the Portuguese to vacate Dadra and Nagar Haveli in 1954. Of them, 55 are alive. Paying tribute to those who passed away in that fight, Shri Purandare appealed to the members of the organisation to continue to organise such functions so that the freedom struggle is not erased from the memory of the people."

In a November 2019 debate on Dadra and Nagar Haveli in Parliament, on a bill that sought to merge the Union territories of Daman and Diu, and Dadra and Nagar Haveli, Union Home Minister Amit Shah said in the Lok Sabha that "many personalities... were behind Dadra Nagar Haveli's liberation from Portugal".

Shah mentioned Babasaheb Purandare, Sudhir Phadke and Sainik School officer Prabhakar Kulkarni among others, and said they played a key role by putting their lives at stake.

According to a PTI report dated 27 November, 2019 on the discussion, "He (Union home minister) said till 1954, the then government did little when

Goa, Daman and Diu and Dadra Nagar Haveli were under Portuguese rule. The young men, he said, then launched an agitation, adding that acclaimed singer Lata Mangeshkar held a programme in Pune to raise funds for the agitation. Shah said Nehru alone should not be credited for the liberation of these areas."

In this context, he was also responding to Trinamool Congress MP Saugata Roy, who had said during the debate that India's first Prime Minister Jawaharlal Nehru should be credited for the region's liberation.

❑

4

Thengadi: An Activist Parliamentarian who Laid the Foundation for 'Atmanirbhar Bharat'

As the Modi government decided to go full throttle on its 'Atmanirbhar Bharat' programme in the post-COVID-19 global and national scenario, few would know, it was an RSS pracharak and an ideological stalwart Dattopant Thengadi who played a key role in shaping this philosophy. Thengadi, was the founder of organisations like Bharatiya Mazdoor Sangh (BMS), Swadeshi Jagran Manch (SJM), Bharatiya Kisan Sangh (BKS) among others.

His ideological influence can be gauged from the fact that the RSS Sarsanghchalak Mohan Bhagwat quoted him in the annual Vijayadashami speech at Nagpur in 2020 when he talked about the conceptual framework of the economic philosophy of 'Swadeshi'. Bhagwat had said, "... Shri Dattopant Thengadiji claimed Swadeshi cuts beyond goods and services and stands for attaining a position of international cooperation by achieving national self-reliance, sovereignty and parity. To achieve financial independence in the future and attain a position of international cooperation we are open to foreign investors and give relaxations to companies offering newer technologies, provided they engage on our terms and mutually agreeable conditions. But such a decision has to be based on mutual consensus."

Bhagwat released a book on 10 November, 2019 in Delhi marking the birth centenary of Thengadi. Interestingly, the book titled 'Dattopant Thengadi: The Activist Parliamentarian' brings out another lesser-known facet of this RSS stalwart that he represented Bharatiya Jana Sangh (BJS) in the Rajya Sabha for two terms from 1964 to 1976. The book has all the speeches or interventions made by Thengadi during his tenure that cover a wide variety of areas from economy and finance to agriculture and cow slaughter.

In the foreword to the book, another RSS stalwart S. Gurumurthy who is well-known for his work on economic issues and who worked with Thengadi during the 1980s and 1990s says, "When globalisation challenged India in the early nineties and every one helplessly just opposed it or blindly welcomed it, he recalled the spirit of the freedom movement, the Swadeshi idea, to show the way to handle it with an indigenous paradigm. In just under 25 years, as Thengadi had predicted, globalisation is over. He waged a war against the WTO. Now the US/West is waging a war against it. It is unfortunate that

Thengadi, who had the conviction that the idea of the nation would prevail over the ideology of globalism is not alive today to hear the President of United States which was the principal driver of globalisation in 1990s, speak 'patriotism, not globalism as the future'. It is again unfortunate that he is not alive to read the Economist magazine which led the intellectual warhorse of globalisation to write the obituary of globalisation titled 'Globalisation is dead'."

Thengadi and Ambedkar

Sharing his personal conversations with Thengadi, Gurumurthy further says, "Thengadi could talk with authority about Babasaheb Ambedkar because he was a full-time understudy with Ambedkar in the last four years of Babasaheb's life. What Thengadi told me was: 'I was an eyewitness to Babasaheb's tensions and problems'. He recalled, 'Babasaheb wanted the Hindu sants (saints) and religious heads to declare openly that untouchability did not have the sanction of Hindu religious scriptures'. RSS efforts in this direction were not bearing fruit. But Babasaheb told Thengadi that time was running out. His health was deteriorating fast in 1954. Babasaheb told Thengadi that 'I have faith in the process of the RSS in removing untouchability. But that is too slow. I cannot wait because I will not live to see the end of the problem'. Thengadi also recalled what made Babasaheb embrace Buddhism, in Babasaheb's own words thus: 'If I did not show the way for this helpless community, they would be hunted down by the Christian church and the communists.' What Babasaheb wanted the Hindu religious leaders to do in 1954, RSS could persuade them to do only a decade later, in 1965, in a conference of Hindu religious leaders in Udupi organised by the Vishva Hindu Parishad. Thengadi's unique knowledge of Babasaheb made many, including me, insist that Thengadi write about his experiences with Babasaheb. A couple of months before he died Thengadi did that, and his book on Babasaheb Ambedkar was also released."

Early Life

Dattopant Bapurao Thengadi was born on 10 November, 1920 in village Arvi of Wardha district in Maharashtra. He finished his post-graduation from Morris College (Nagpur) and his LLB from Law College Nagpur. In 1940, when MS Golwalkar became the second Sarsanghchalak, he gave a clarion call to the youth to become RSS pracharaks (full-time workers) to expand the organisation's work. Responding to the call, Thengadi joined the RSS as a pracharak in 1942 and remained so till he passed away at the age of 84 on 14 October, 2004. In addition to his well-known organisational roles, he is also remembered by many as the energetic and deft Organising Secretary of BJS for Madhya Pradesh during 1952-1953 and for South India during 1956-57. He was associated with the formation of many Sangh-inspired organisations like Akhil Bharatiya Vidyarthi Parishad (ABVP), BJS, Bharatiya Kisan Sangh, Swadeshi Jagaran Manch, Akhil Bharatiya Grahak Panchayat, Samskar Bharati, Akhil

Bharatiya Adhivakta Parishad, Samajik Samrasata Manch, Bharatiya Vichar Kendram. He wrote several books. One of his most popular books that gives the blueprint of 'Swadeshi' economics is 'Third Way'.

❑

5

Ashok Singhal: The Man who Steered the Movement to Build the Ram Temple

Even as the much-awaited construction of Ram Temple started on 5 August 2020, one of the key leaders whose contribution to the successful culmination of this movement must be recalled is Ashok Singhal.

Singhal can be credited with creating a groundswell of support for the Ram Janmabhoomi movement by taking it out from a limited sphere of religious leaders to the masses through his extraordinary organisational skills which he had developed working at the grassroots level as an RSS pracharak for almost three decades.

Having a degree in Metallurgical Engineering did not deviate him from becoming a pracharak of Rashtriya Swayamsevak Sangh in 1950 though his father was initially reluctant to let him go. He dedicated the next 65 years of his life to the organisation and the cause to which he remained fiercely committed that included the single-minded pursuit to build a Ram Temple at the birth place of Lord Rama.

After becoming an RSS pracharak in 1950, Singhal initially worked for around 25 years in different districts of Uttar Pradesh as district pracharak. Initially, he was entrusted with organisational work in Gorakhpur and was subsequently sent to Varanasi to carry out the same work.

From 1952 to 1958 he was district pracharak of Saharanpur. In 1958 he was sent to Kanpur and in 1963 he became a sambhag pracharak overseeing organisational work in several districts. After that he kept on working in different parts of the country and with various other organisations inspired by the RSS including ABVP, a student organisation.

In 1975, he participated in the anti-Emergency movement and was jailed. At that time, he was working with ABVP. After the Emergency, he came out of the prison and was given the responsibility of prant pracharak of Delhi RSS. This was a turning point for him as he catapulted to the centre stage in the wake of the action plan initiated by him after conversion of Dalits into Islam at Meenakshipuram in Tamil Nadu that had become a major issue of debate.

He spearheaded an organisation called Virat Hindu Samaj as general secretary to respond to the Meenakshipuram incident. This newly formed organisation gave a call for a massive public rally in Delhi where around five lakh Hindus gathered to protest this conversion.

This was followed by similar conferences, rallies and public meetings all over the country forcing the then Congress government to take up the issue of conversion in the Parliament where all major political parties condemned attempts to convert Hindus and asked the government to take appropriate steps.

Singhal was also a major catalyst for setting up 'Single Teacher Schools', an educational project of the Vishva Hindu Parishad (VHP). These schools operate in the remotest areas of the country where young children are not able to get educated due to geographical challenges curtailing their access to basic schooling. At present, around one lakh such schools, run by the VHP, are functional imparting education to millions of children every year.

In 1982, he was appointed joint general secretary of Vishva Hindu Parishad (VHP). The VHP was set up in 1964 and was working largely to bring various Hindu sects together to unite Hindus and end discrimination based on caste, and creating a network of Hindus living abroad.

In 1986 after Har Mohan Lal, a senior VHP leader passed away, Singhal was entrusted with the crucial responsibility of being its general secretary. It may be mentioned here that 1986 to 1992 was the peak of the Ram Janmabhoomi movement and it was Singhal who was playing a key role in expanding the base of the organisation through various programmes, one of the most important being 'Shila Pujan'. The bricks for foundation of the proposed Ram Temple were sent from all across the country to Ayodhya. This resulted in creating a massive support base for this movement at the grassroots level, especially in the rural India.

Singhal played a lead role in shaping the Ram Janmabhoomi movement right since the first gathering of Hindu religious and spiritual leaders in 1984 at Vigyan Bhavan, in New Delhi where the matter of reconstruction of Hindu temples at Ayodhya, Mathura and Kashi (Varanasi) were formally taken up.

He ensured that any possible fissures amongst various Hindu sects do not mar the progress of the movement. An organiser par excellence, he led the movement for Kar Seva at Ayodhya in 1991 from the front when the then Uttar Pradesh Chief Minister Mulayam Singh Yadav ordered firing on Kar Sevaks.

Ashok Singhal was born on 27 September, 1926 in Agra. His father Mahavir Singh was a Deputy Collector and his mother's name was Vidyawati. He had six brothers and one sister. In 1950, Ashok Singhal passed out from Banaras Hindu University (BHU) with degree of Engineering in Metallurgy. He had got associated with the RSS during his childhood in Prayag and had decided to dedicate his life for the organisation. All his brothers were RSS swayamsevaks and used to attend its Shakha.

Ashok Singhal's initial contact in Prayag was with Professor Rajendra Singh also known as Rajju bhaiya. The latter became the fourth RSS Sarsanghchalak in 1994.

Singhal was the president of the VHP from 2005–2011 and then became a mentor of the organisation till he passed away on 17 November, 2015 after a brief illness. However, till his last breath, he continued to pursue the cause of building a Ram Temple at Ayodhya.

❑

6

How Rest of the World Looks at 'Rama' and His Story

With the dust of disputes having settled over the existence and birth of Shri Rama, whose temple is being constructed at Ayodhya now in the Bharatiya state of Uttar Pradesh followed by 500 years of struggle by Hindus and a Supreme Court decision after a protracted legal battle in Indian courts, it is probably time to take a look at the expanse of Rama's influence that transcends borders and time.

As early as A.D. 251, K'ang Seng Hui rendered the Jataka form of the 'Ramayana' into Chinese and, in A.D. 472, another Chinese translation was prepared of the 'Nidana of Dashratha Jataka' from a lost Sanskrit text, by Kekaya.

In the sixth century, the Simhala poet-king, Kumaradasa, composed the 'Janakiharana', the earliest Sanskrit work of Ceylon. In the seventh century in Cambodia, Khmer citation attested to the popularity of the 'Ramayana', the story of Rama. An inscription declared that a certain Somasharman presented the

'Ramayana', the 'Purana' and the complete 'Bharata' to a temple.

Towards the close of the ninth century, an east Iranian version of the Ramayana appeared in Khotanese, an Iranian dialect. The story of Rama spread in the northernmost lands of Asia from Tibet, where it was found in two versions in manuscripts of the seventh–ninth centuries.

"The oldest manuscript of the Ramayana of Valmiki, dated A.D. 1075, is preserved in Nepal," writes Meenakshi Jain, noted historian in her seminal work 'Rama and Ayodhya'. "The Rama story occurred in three early Buddhist texts—the 'Dasharath Kathanam', the 'Anamakam Jatakam' and the 'Dashrath Jataka'. The 'Dasharath Kathanam', the earliest, belongs to the first-second century A.D.," says Jain.

William Finch, the European traveller (1608–11), who visited Ayodhya, has written in his travel account that "Rama was born in the human form to see the tamasha (theatrics) of the world."

Noted author and traveller Thomas Herbert described in his published work, 'Some Yeares Travels into Divers Parts of Asia and Afrique' about Rama's significance and influence—"Ducerat (Dashrath), who begat Rama, a king so famous for piety and high attempts, that to this day his name is exceedingly honoured, so that when they say Ram-Ram, 'tis as if they should say 'all good betide you'." That is, according to Thomas Herbert, all good will fall on you. From addressing Ram-Ram it is expected that all good would fall on the caller and listener.

French traveller Jean de Thevenot also wrote a book based on his travels in India in the year 1666 A.D. The book was translated in English and published in London in the year 1687 A.D. He wrote in 'The Travels of Monsieur de Thevenot' about Rama, "The Indians render him divine honours in their pagodas and elsewhere; and when they salute their friends they repeat his name, saying 'Ram Ram'. Their adoration consists in joining their hands, as if they prayed, letting them fall very low, and then lifting them up again gently to their mouth, and last of all, in raising them over their heads."

'A Voyage to Surrat', in the year 1689, written by JO Vington also describes a practice bythe Hindus of incessantly chanting 'Ram-Ram' during their funeral. Another description came from Joseph Tieffenthaler's written accounts in the form of the book, 'Descriptio Indiae', i.e., 'Description of India'. The Austrian Jesuit priest, who stayed in Avadh (1766–71) had lived in India for more than two decades and he was well-versed in both Persian and Sanskrit.

Tieffenthaler visited Ayodhya (then known as Fyzabad) and travelled the whole of Avadh (known as Oudh during that era) during 1766–1771. Its appearance in 1770 is thus described by Tieffenthaler: "Avad called Adjudea by the learned Hindoos, is city of the highest antiquity...The most remarkable place is that which is called Sorgodoari, that is to say, the heavenly temple because they say that Rama carried away from thence to heaven all the inhabitants of the city."

"On the 24th of the month Tshet (Choitru) a large concourse of people celebrate here the birthday of Rama, so famous throughout India," he added.

A French scholar by the name of C. Mentelle also wrote about Ayodhya in great detail in his book, 'Courses of Cosmography (Cosmology) on Geography, on Chronology and on Ancient and Modern History'. "Avadh, also known as Aoude and Oude in our country (France), and the learned Indian name it Adjudea, is one of the most ancient cities, situated on the banks of the River Ghagra and we consider that the tenth incarnation of Lord Vishnu happened in this city, in the form of Ramaji, whose father was the king of Avadh. The Indians come here from far off places on a big pilgrimage. In those days at Ayodhya there was an edifice called the celestial temple, from where it is said that Ramaji had taken to the heaven all the inhabitants of the city. This temple and several others were destroyed."

In A.D. 1783, William Hodges visited Ayodhya and made a beautiful sketch of Ayodhya on the Saryu ghat (bank of Saryu River). In A.D. 1789, William Daniells visited Ayodhya and made certain sketches.

❑

7

'Warrior Sadhu' to Kothari Brothers: 10 Unsung Heroes of Ayodhya Ram Mandir Movement

There have been several unsung heroes of the movement to build a Ram Temple at the birthplace of Lord Ram in Ayodhya, Uttar Pradesh, in the post-Independence era, especially during the 1980s and early 1990s.

The 'Warrior Sadhu' who put an idol of Lord Ram at the disputed site in 1949, a former Congress leader credited with preparing the ground for the movement, two brothers from Calcutta (now Kolkata) who came to Ayodhya to perform the kar seva (volunteer service) and were killed in police firing—there have been many who are to be remembered for their contribution.

Here is a look at a few of them.

Bairagi Abhiram Das

Born in Darbhanga, Bihar, Bairagi Abhiram Das was an ascetic from the Ramanandi sect and his name cropped up after an idol of Lord Ram emerged at the disputed structure on Ram's birthplace on the intervening night of 22–23 December 1949. He was made the prime accused in the First Information Report (FIR) lodged by the administration at the time.

He was known as the 'Warrior Sadhu' in Ayodhya. A member of the Hindu Mahasabha, Das was well-built and well-versed in the art of wrestling. He died in 1981.

Devraha Baba

Known to be a highly spiritual ascetic, the details about his birthplace and year remain a mystery. He stayed on the banks of Saryu River near Deoria in Uttar Pradesh. His followers included the first President of India Dr Rajendra Prasad, and leaders like Indira Gandhi, Rajiv Gandhi and Atal Bihari Vajpayee.

He presided over the 'Dharma Sansad' in January 1984 at Kumbh in Prayagraj where a decision was taken collectively by Hindu religious and spiritual leaders cutting across sects to lay the foundation stone of a Ram Temple in Ayodhya on 9 November, 1989. It is said that when Rajiv Gandhi went to seek his advice and blessings regarding laying of the foundation stone, Devraha Baba told him, "Bachcha, ho jane do" (Son, let it happen).

Moropant Pingle

A graduate from Morris College of Nagpur and a pracharak of the RSS, Pingle was the 'invisible' key strategist, who played a crucial role in initiating all the major 'yatras' and countrywide campaigns, including the 'Shila Pujan' programme, under which more than 3 lakh bricks were sent to Ayodhya.

Pingle always preferred to work behind the scenes and was a key strategist for building the temple movement in the 1980s.

Mahant Avaidyanath

Avaidyanath was the first president of the Ram Janmabhoomi Mukti Yagya Samiti set up in the mid-1980s to lead the Ram Temple movement. He was the president of another key organisation—Ram Janmabhoomi Nyas Samiti—that played a crucial role in this movement.

Born as Kripa Singh Bisht, he became a follower of Mahant Digvijaynath of Gorakshapeeth in Uttar Pradesh and took up the name of Mahant Avaidyanath in 1940 as an ascetic.

In 1969, he became the head of the Gorakshapeeth. He was also a member of the Hindu Mahasabha. He was a five-term MLA and was a four-term Lok Sabha MP from Gorakhpur. He was made one of the accused in the Babri Masjid demolition case.

Swami Vamdev

A soft-spoken ascetic, who was deeply committed to the cause of cow protection, Vamdev played a key role in bringing various Hindu religious and spiritual leaders together at one platform through an all India-level meet in Jaipur in 1984.

More than 400 Hindu religious leaders brainstormed for 15 days to put together the future roadmap of the movement. Swami Vamdev led the kar sevaks (volunteers) from the front in 1990 in Ayodhya when several of them were killed in police firing ordered by the Mulayam Singh Yadav government. Despite his old age, he was present in Ayodhya on 6 December 1992 when the Babri Masjid was pulled down.

Shrish Chandra Dikshit

Dikshit was a frontline leader of the Ram Janmabhoomi movement in the 1980s. He was the director general of police in Uttar Pradesh from 1982 to 1984. After his retirement, he joined the Vishva Hindu Parishad as its vice-president.

He played a key role in strategising the movement of kar sevaks in Ayodhya and working out the finer details for various on-ground campaigns run by the VHP. He was arrested in 1990 for participating in Ram Janmabhoomi movement during the kar seva in Ayodhya. He was elected as a Member of Parliament from the Varanasi constituency in 1991 on a BJP ticket. Varanasi is now represented by Prime Minister Narendra Modi.

Vishnu Hari Dalmia

A scion of a well-known industrialist family, Dalmia

was the president of the VHP from 1992 to 2005. Known for keeping a low profile, Dalmia was one of the key leaders of the Ram Janmabhoomi movement.

When Shri Ram Janmabhoomi Nyas was set up in 1985, he was made its treasurer. He was arrested after the demolition of the Babri Masjid.

Daudayal Khanna

As the general secretary of Ram Janmabhoomi Mukti Yagna Samiti, Daudayal Khanna played a key role in preparing the ground for the movement.

He was a Congress leader in his early years and was the health minister in the Congress-led government in Uttar Pradesh in the 1960s. He was the one who brought up the issue of reconstructing temples in Ayodhya, Mathura and Kashi (Varanasi) at a public meeting in 1983. His initiative proved to be the key catalyst in restarting the Ram Janmabhoomi movement. In September 1984, he led one of the first 'yatras' of this movement from Sitamarhi, Bihar.

Kothari Brothers

Ram Kumar Kothari and Sharad Kumar Kothari were siblings, who came to Ayodhya from Kolkata for the kar seva in October 1990.

They participated in the kar seva in Ayodhya on 30 October, 1990 as members of the first batch of kar sevaks. Two days later, on 2 November, both of them were shot dead from point-blank range by the police when they were performing kar seva. Ram was 23 and Sharad was just 20 years old when they were killed.

The killing of the Kothari brothers outraged Hindus across the country, and they were treated as the heroes and martyrs of the Ram Janmabhoomi movement. In the 1990s, their deaths drew a large number of youth to this movement.

(All inputs for this article have been sourced from VHP archives and 'Yudh Mein Ayodhya' by Hemant Sharma, Prabhat Prakashan).

❑

8

Goswami Tulsidas: A Pioneer of Hindu Renaissance

As Ayodhya witnessed beginning of the construction of a Ram Temple on 5 August 2020, ending centuries of wait, the day almost coincided with the birth anniversary of the person who can be called the original catalyst for the Ram Janmabhoomi movement.

It is Hindu saint and poet Goswami Tulsidas' epochal work, 'Ramcharitmanas', which is credited with taking the story of Lord Ram to every household in north and central India, creating an emotional connect between an average Hindu household and Lord Ram.

That ultimately proved to be the key factor in building a movement for the construction of the Ram Temple in Ayodhya, the birth place of Ram, after over four centuries. The movement gained momentum when the VHP took over the mantle to build a nationwide movement.

Before he wrote 'Ramcharitmanas' in the local Hindi dialect called Awadhi around 400 years ago, the story of Lord Rama was largely recited in Sanskrit in northern and central India through Valmiki's 'Ramayana'. But Tulsidas, despite being a Sanskrit scholar, chose Awadhi. He began writing it in Ayodhya and finished it in Kashi (Varanasi).

The birth anniversary of Goswami Tulsidas was on Monday, 27 July 2020, just a week before the construction work for the Ram Temple was set to begin formally.

Philip Lutgendorf, an American Indologist and professor of Hindi and Modern Indian Studies in the US, says in his seminal work, 'The Life of a Text: Performing the Ramcaritmanas of Tulsidas', that anyone interested in the religion and culture of Northern India invariably encounters a reference to the 'Ramcharitmanas'.

"This sixteenth-century retelling of the legend of Ram by the poet Tulsidas has been hailed not merely as the greatest modern Indian epic, but as something like a living sum of Indian culture," wrote Lutgendorf, who is considered to be one of the foremost experts on the 'Ramcharitmanas'.

He wrote, "The tallest tree in the magic garden of medieval Hindu poesy", was acclaimed by Mahatma Gandhi as "the greatest book of all devotional literature."

Western observers have christened it "the Bible of Northern India" and called it "the best and most trustworthy guide to the popular living faith of its people."

The time of Tulsidas

There are different versions about the place and year of birth of Tulsidas, ranging from 1497 to 1532. But there is unanimity that he was born at one of the places that is currently part of Uttar Pradesh during the month of Shravana, according to the Hindu calendar.

Tulsidas Jayanti is observed on the Saptami of the Krishna Paksha, i.e., the seventh day of the dark fortnight of the moon.

Tulsidas wrote around a dozen texts on Lord Ram's life—the two most popular being 'Ramcharitmanas' and 'Hanuman Chalisa' (40 verses in praise of Lord Hanuman). The massive following of Lord Hanuman today can be attributed to the latter.

The poet himself founded a large number of Hanuman temples and is known to have set up a large number of 'akharas' with Lord Hanuman's statue being enshrined there. The tradition continues even today as all the Indian 'akharas', in north and central India, have a statue of Lord Hanuman.

Some of the unknown feats of Tulsidas include his initiation of Ramleela (theatrical performance of Lord Ram's story) across the region. The tradition of holding Ramleela for nine days prior to the festival of Vijayadashami (Dussehra) still holds strong not only in India but also in several countries of south-east Asia.

The popular appeal of 'Ramcharitmanas' can be gauged from the fact that when migrant labourers were moved during the British rule from India to

Mauritius, Fiji, Suriname and many other countries, they carried with them the rich tradition of reciting the epic and performing Ramleela, which has thrived there over the time.

A pioneer of Hindu renaissance

Tulsidas is in fact one of the most understated pioneers of Hindu renaissance in medieval India. "The legend suggests Tulsi's success at transcending sectarian differences and at synthesizing diverse strands of the Hindu tradition," Lutgendorf wrote.

Indologist and British Civil Servant FS Growse noted in 'The Ramayana of Tulsidas' (1883) the overarching impact of the poet.

"There are Vallabhacharis and Radha-Vallabhis and Maluk Dasis and Pran Nathis, and so on, in interminable succession, but there are no Tulsidasis," he wrote. "Virtually, however, the whole of Vaishnava Hinduism has fallen under his sway; for the principles that he expounded have permeated every sect and explicitly or implicitly now form the nucleus of the popular faith as it prevails throughout the whole of the Bengal Presidency from Haridwar to Calcutta."

In the medieval era, when Hindu society was struggling with several divisions and facing an onslaught from Islamic invaders, according to Lutgendorf, 'Ramcharitmanas' played a key role in uniting the Hindu society.

"Reconciliation and synthesis are indeed the

underlying themes of Tulsi's epic: the reconciliation of Vaishnavism and Shaivism through a henotheistic vision that advocates worshipping Shiva as father of the Universe while making him the archetypal devotee of Ram," Lutgendorf wrote. "A similar rapprochement is effected between the nirgun and sagun traditions—between worship of a formless God and of a God with attributes."

"His hero is at once Valmiki's exemplary prince, the cosmic Vishnu of the 'Puranas', and the transcendent brahman of the Advaitins," Lutgendorf added. "What weaves together such 'inconsistent' theological strands is the overwhelming devotional mood of the poem, expressing fervent love for the divine through poetry of the most captivating musicality."

Frank Whaling says in his 'The Rise of the Religious Significance of Rama' (1980) that Tulsidas created "an integral rather than a new symbol" of Lord Rama.

❑

9

Sino-Indian Battle of Narratives: Maxwell vs Lintner

As the relationship between India and China evolved especially in the wake of the 1962 war between the two countries, China waged another global battle throughout these years against India. It is the 'battle of narratives' and unfortunately we seem to have hardly fought it well enough.

After 1962, China painstakingly built a narrative that hinged on the key argument that the then Prime Minister Jawaharlal Nehru's policy of setting up forward posts on the border areas led to this conflict. Commonly known as 'forward policy,' China was able to convince all the major countries over the years that it was India which provoked the war and not China. Unfortunately, we failed to notice this and those who noticed it did not seem to have done enough to counter it.

What really helped to propel the Chinese version of events in 1962 to become the global narrative and misguide the global opinion was Anglo-Australian journalist Neville Maxwell's book 'India's China War'. The book was first published in 1970 and has been treated as the most authentic work on the 1962 war.

The impact of Maxwell's book can be gauged from the fact that in 1971, at an official banquet in Beijing, Chinese Premier Zhou Enlai and Pakistan's Prime Minister Zulfikar Ali Bhutto kept aside all protocols when they got up from the head table and walked to the table where foreign correspondents including Maxwell were sitting. Zhou told Maxwell through his interpreter that Maxwell's book has greatly benefitted China and then he went on to raise a toast to him.

US Secretary of State Henry Kissinger, while visiting Beijing in the 1970s, acknowledged that after reading Maxwell's book, he was convinced that the US could do business with China. Kissinger, in fact, convinced US President Nixon to agree with Maxwell's theory when it came to the 1962 war.

It took more than five and a half decades to counter this vicious propaganda against India unleashed by Maxwell's book and then further promoted by another Western intellectual Alistair Campbell through his books and writings on India and China. Ironically, it was not an Indian author but Swedish journalist Bertil Lintner who wrote the most balanced and authentic account of 1962 war. His book 'China's India War: Collision Course on the Roof of the World' is a repository of facts and exposes Maxwell's agenda-driven book. This is the first real salvo against the Chinese propaganda machine through all these years.

Lintner rips apart Maxwell's arguments and the Chinese propaganda as he mentions, "Maxwell believes that the likeliest date of the decision by the Chinese to attack seems to lie in mid-October 1962 because India had established an outpost at a place called Dhola and escalated tension at the Eastern sector of the border which until then had been dormant."

"It is uncertain whether Maxwell is deliberately feigning ignorance of the Chinese build-up across and along the McMahon Line which began shortly after the Lhasa revolt in 1959 or whether he is unaware of it. No serious military analyst would conclude that the decision to go to war with India on such a massive scale as occurred on 20 October, 1962 or even the fighting that took place during the days before that would have been taken only a week or even a couple of weeks before the PLA crossed the McMahon Line in the east as well as the Line of Actual Control in Ladakh, 3000 kilometres to the west.

Chinese preparations for the war began long before October 1962 and the November 1961 meeting where Nehru had outlined his Forward policy."

Lintner argues, "It is also important to remember that the 1962 war had nothing to do with the establishment of an Indian Army post in one of the remotest corners of the subcontinent. That could be seen as a pretext, but even then at best, a rather flimsy one. Mao Zedong had told the Nepalese and the Soviet delegations before and after the war that the issue was never the McMohan Line or the border dispute.

China thought that India had designs for Tibet, which, in the 1950s, was being integrated into Mao's People's Republic."

Thus, China had planned the invasion much earlier. Lintner reveals in his book, "At a meeting on 25th March 1959 only three weeks after the outbreak of the Lhasa uprising and as the Dalai Lama was on his way over the mountains to India, Deng Xiaoping, then a political as well as a military leader made China's position clear; 'When the time comes, we will certainly settle accounts with them (the Indians). And according to Bruce Riedel, one of America's leading experts on US security as well as South Asian issues, ...as early as 1959 Mao decided that he would have to take firm action against Nehru."

Lintner challenges the fundamental premise on which Maxwell has built his arguments i.e., the Henderson Brooks-Bhagat Report. He writes, "One would need to have a lot of imagination to conclude from the Henderson Brooks- Bhagat Report that India was the aggressor and China the aggrieved party in 1962. The question of who attacked whom for determining who was responsible for the war was not even within the scope of the enquiry which had been set up to look into four specific aspects of the war that could explain the Indian defeat: possible shortcomings in training and recruitment; the system of command; the physical fitness of the troops; and the capacity of commanders at all levels to influence their subordinates.

In essence the Henderson Brooks-Bhagat Report states little more than that. India was ill-prepared for the war and therefore unable to withstand the Chinese assault over the Himalayas. It also points out weaknesses in India's command structure and the lack of effective cooperation between the government and the military. It certainly does not say that India was responsible for the war not does it question the Forward Policy per se."

❑

10

Forgotten War of 1967: When India Thrashed China

The clashes between Indian and Chinese soldiers often happen. In this context it would be pertinent to mention that whenever there is tension on the border between India and China, the 1962 war emerges as a reference point for us. If we look at the history of India-China relations, the tragedy is that we remember 1962 but we have forgotten 1967. The 1967 war needs to be recalled today.

It all began on 11 September 1967. As the day began, some Indian soldiers went to lay down barbed wire to strengthen security at the border at a place called Nathu La in Sikkim. About 100 Chinese soldiers arrived and threatened the Indians. But Indian soldiers continued their work. Chinese soldiers went back to their bunkers and started firing at 7.45 am with light machine guns. Shortly thereafter, Chinese artillery attacked Indian outposts and bunkers.

But it was not 1962. This time the Indians did not have a shortage of weapons nor was their morale weak. Some Indian soldiers were martyred in this initial deceptive attack by China. The Indians fired back. But the Chinese military did not suffer as much. Several hours had passed since the war started but the Indian cannons were still silent. The command was with Lieutenant-General Sagat Singh and at that time it was required to get permission from the central government in Delhi if Indian soldiers wanted to use artillery. The day was advancing, Indian casualties were rising, the Chinese army was consolidating its position. Ultimately, Sagat Singh decided that this time he would not let 1962 repeat, instead he was going to write a new chapter in history. He himself stood on the battlefield and ordered the artillery to start pounding the Chinese positions.

Within a few hours, the scene of the battlefield changed. The Indian artillery was placed in a much better tactical position as they were stationed at Sebu La and Camel's Back from where the entire Yatung Valley was within their firing range where the Chinese were stationed. The Indian artillery attack uprooted the Chinese, destroyed their posts and destroyed their communication lines. What was left on the Chinese side was nothing but corpses in the bunkers. About 350 Chinese soldiers were killed and more than 450 were injured.

The Indian army had taken the revenge for the defeat of 1962. The Chinese army's ego had been crushed. So it hit back and tried to corner Indians in a place called Cho La, again at Sikkim border. This incident took place in the same sector within 15 days after the battle of Nathu La. The result was that the Indian and Chinese forces clashed once again. This time too, the command of the Indian Army was in the hands of Sagat Singh and China suffered heavy losses. China first attacked some Indian soldiers by deceit. But after this the Indian troops retaliated in such a ferocious way that China had to retreat and attempts to capture Cho La failed. The bravery of the Indian soldiers can be gauged from an example. Gurkha soldier Devi Prasad Limbu, without caring for his life in the initial attack, had severed the head of five Chinese soldiers by a single attack with a Khukri, a traditional Gurkha knife. Surprised by his valour, when the Chinese military officer handed over his body to the Indian authorities, he admitted that he had read stories of such bravery but saw it with his own eyes for the first time. The Chinese themselves gave him the title of 'The Tiger of Cho La'.

Massive defeats in two major conflicts and that too within a month were big psychological blows to China. It also helped Indian forces to recover from the shock of the 1962 defeat.

It is to be noted that due to this bravery of Sagat Singh and valour of Indian soldiers, India secured the strategically important sites—Nathu La and Cho La—under its jurisdiction. Due to the presence of the Indian Army especially at Nathu La, China could not come forward openly in support of Pakistan in the Indo-Pakistan War of 1971.

Had China won the battle of Nathu La, it would

have had direct access to the Siliguri corridor which connects North East India with the rest of India. If Nathu La had been captured by China, during 1971 war, it could have pressurised India using the Siliguri corridor. It would have facilitated it to establish contact with the Pakistani forces in East Pakistan very easily and the rest of India might have been cut off from this part of the country. But India's victory over China in the 1967 war eliminated the possibility of any interference by China in the Siliguri corridor, thus leaving India in a strategically advantageous position.

The victory of India in this 1967 war had far-reaching strategic consequences. After this, there was no major conflict with China for more than six decades. China had got the message that India was not going to repeat the mistakes of 1962 and would respond strategically in an effective manner. It is unfortunate that many books were written, films were made and hundreds of articles etc. written, even at present, on the defeat of India in 1962. But the glorious victory of 1967 has been confined to a handful of newspaper clippings.

❑

11

India's China Policy: What Nehru and others could Learn from RSS

The Rashtriya Swayamsevak Sangh (RSS) has always favoured a firm and strong China Policy. It has been consistently pursuing this since the 1950s. However now, along with strategic component, the economic component has also been added to it, to make it more effective as several organisations inspired by the RSS are focussing on boycotting Chinese goods.

The RSS has consistently taken the stand that India should be wary of China and has urged the successive governments not to let their guard down when it comes to China. It also holds responsible the Congress government led by Jawaharlal Nehru for the 1962 debacle in war with China.

An RSS resolution passed in 2012 said, "It is universally acknowledged that the debacle of 1962 was essentially the making of the political and diplomatic leadership of our country. Warnings by several eminent people including Sardar Patel (Sardar

Vallabhbhai Patel) and Shri Guruji (the second RSS Sarsanghchalak) were unheeded to by the then leadership which went about with its romantic world view totally ignoring the ground situation. China had annexed Tibet first and then launched aggression on our territory."

The RSS, in fact, has been quite vocal about China since the 1950s and had always favoured a strong 'China Policy' to check China's expansionist tendencies. Addressing a public rally in Ramlila Maidan in Delhi on 23 December, 1962, the second Sarsanghchalak of RSS, MS Golwalkar, also known as Shri Guruji ('Shri Guruji Samagra', Volume 10, Pp160-166, Suruchi Prakashan) had said, "One of the key reasons for China's expansionist policies lies in the fact that it ruled by a Communist regime and 'Expansionism is a key characteristic of Communism.'"

Interestingly, despite being critical of the then Prime Minister Jawaharlal Nehru's China Policy, he urged all the political parties to keep their differences aside and support the Nehru government in the war effort against China. "We must remove all.... Political differences right now and remember only one thing that we are fighting a war against an enemy and we should stand as One nation."

On 5 November, 1962, amidst the war with China, Guruji issued a statement in Nagpur that proves to be even more relevant today ('Shri Guruji Samagra', Volume 10, Pp 156-159, Suruchi Prakashan). He cautioned the Nehru government that China would try to use Nepal against India so, "We must establish very close and cordial relationships with Nepal....if we don't succeed in this, our difficulties are going to increase."

On the eve of the 50th anniversary of the 1962 war between India and China, the RSS had passed a resolution in 2012 in Chennai. The resolution was passed in the meeting of Akhil Bharatiya Karyakari Mandal (AKBM), one of the highest bodies for policy formulation and decision-making in the organisation.

The resolution lays bare the RSS' perspective on China Policy. Expressing deep concern about China, the resolution emphasised the urgent 'need for a Comprehensive National Security Policy vis-a-vis China.'

The resolution said, "China has strategically built and upgraded its border infrastructure along Bharat-Tibet border that includes a network of air bases, missile launching pads, cantonments and other physical infrastructure. The ABKM calls upon our Government that in view of the enhanced threats from the aggressive manoeuvres of China along the border Bharat also should invest adequately in border management and security preparedness."

"Modern wars are not necessarily fought only on the borders. We need to develop comprehensive military technological superiority keeping in view the rapid strides China has made in this field," it added.

Much in advance to the challenges which we are witnessing today when it comes to the technology footprint of China creating challenges for India's national security as well as the efforts to go swadeshi, the RSS had warned in this 2012 resolution, "The deep penetration of China in vital sectors like energy, information and communication technology, industry and commerce in Bharat and its designs to divert our river waters are a serious cause of concern."

"The ABKM underscores the threat from China in the field of cyber technology and communications. China has invested heavily in developing strong cyber warfare capability using which it can cripple the technological capabilities of even the advanced countries like the US. Those countries are also concerned about this threat from China and are taking counter measures. While our advances in hi-tech areas are noteworthy, the ABKM urges the Government should give necessary importance to augmenting our cyber-security capability also," it added.

Explaining further the RSS' stand on the 'China Policy' of India, the resolution said, "Bharat has always strived to maintain good relations with various countries. About two decades ago we exhorted a new Look East Policy thereby trying to establish closer relations with countries to our East and South-East. We have all along been the champions of peace in the world. In order for us to achieve these lofty ideals the ABKM urges the Government that it should learn lessons from the 1962 experience and give highest priority to developing a comprehensive national security policy vis-a-vis China."

❑

12

Syama Prasad Mookerjee: Sacrificing Life for Jammu & Kashmir

The death anniversary of Dr Syama Prasad Mookerjee, the founder of Bharatiya Jana Sangh, held a special significance in 2019. The cause for which he sacrificed his life has finally reached a logical conclusion around six-and-a-half decades after his death.

On 5 August 2019, the Narendra Modi government amended Article 370 and removed the contentious Section 35A, paving the way for all provisions of the Constitution to be extended to Jammu and Kashmir.

The now bifurcated state does not have a separate flag anymore, one of the key issues raised by Mookerjee.

What we witnessed in August 2019 was the culmination of the clarion call given by Dr Mookerjee—“Ek desh mein do Vidhan, do nishan nahin chalenge, nahin chalenge (Two Constitutions and two flags in one country are not acceptable)." He also launched the first satyagraha on the issue in the post-Independence era, which attracted a huge number of people.

Mookerjee, a leader from West Bengal, was a member of Nehru's cabinet until he resigned in 1950 to protest the Nehru-Liaquat Pact, a treaty meant to secure the security and rights of minorities in both countries.

The Jana Sangh founder then became one of the most vocal critics of Nehru and associated himself with the Jammu and Kashmir issue, for which he ultimately sacrificed his life— Mookerjee died in Srinagar on 23 June under mysterious circumstances.

It all began in April 1952 when Prem Nath Dogra, a leader of the Praja Parishad Party of Jammu and Kashmir, visited New Delhi and met Mookerjee, urging him to help with the ongoing agitation in the state.

The Parishad's key demand was that Jammu and Kashmir's accession to India should be finalised through a resolution adopted by the state's Constituent Assembly. It demanded that the state should adopt the provisions of the Constitution of India related to fundamental rights, citizenship, financial integration, Supreme Court, Emergency powers of President and abolition of customs duty, conduct of elections and acceptance of supremacy of Indian flag and policy regarding liberation and occupation of Pakistan-held territory.

Mookerjee suggested that Prem Nath Dogra put all

the facts before Nehru. Dogra tried to meet Nehru, but could not secure an appointment.

Mookerjee in Jammu & Kashmir

Disappointed over the developments in Delhi, Dogra went back and under his leadership, the Praja Parishad decided to hold a convention of its workers in Jammu on 9–10 August 1952. He invited several MPs and senior political leaders from Delhi, including Mookerjee.

The Jana Sangh founder addressed a mammoth public meeting in Jammu where he gave the famous clarion call for one Constitution.

During this visit, he also met Sheikh Abdullah and had a long talk with him, but there was no positive breakthrough. In the beginning of December 1952, Praja Parishad started a peaceful satyagraha in Jammu and Kashmir. The movement was supported by the Bharatiya Jana Sangh.

In support of this movement, Mookerjee decided to write letters to Nehru after the first annual session of BJS from 29 to 31 December 1952.

Meanwhile, the situation deteriorated in Jammu and Kashmir. Mookerjee received many letters about the atrocities in the state. On 27 February 1953, Durga Das Verma, general secretary of Praja Parishad in Jammu, sent him a telegram, copies of which were also sent to many other political leaders in Delhi as well as the President, the PM and the home minister of India.

"Merciless and shameless beating of Doctor Om Prakash, president, City Parishad; Shri Gopal Dass, publicity secretary, and four others by the authorities. Forced removal to Srinagar insulting and intimidating; Gopal Dass arm fractured," the telegram read. "Hunger strike since five days. Public sentiments are running high. Pray intervention."

A day before this telegram, a meeting of the leaders of the BJS, the Hindu Mahasabha and the Akali Dal was held in Delhi and it was decided that 5 March 1953 will be observed as "Jammu and Kashmir Day" throughout the country in support of the agitation by the Praja Parishad in the erstwhile state.

On that day, Mookerjee attended a public meeting at Company Bagh in New Delhi where he said a joint committee had decided that a satyagraha would be started, over the Praja Parishad's demands, both in Delhi and at Pathankot in addition to other districts of Punjab.

On 6 March, another meeting was held in Delhi on the same issue for which Mookerjee was arrested for violating prohibitory orders under Section 144. He was, however, released by the Supreme Court.

The J&K Satyagraha

As the satyagraha began, Mookerjee began travelling extensively. He addressed several well-attended public meetings and press conferences in several cities and towns, including Delhi, Jaipur, Ajmer, Bhopal, Gwalior and Indore.

The intelligence reports of the home ministry had then clearly said the satyagraha attracted a fairly large crowd (National Archives of India, D.I.B. reports–Praja Parishad agitation in Delhi. New Delhi: Ministry of States f.no. 8, (20)-k/53).

Mookerjee finally realised that he was left with no other option but to visit Jammu & Kashmir. He left Delhi by train on 8 May 1953. While travelling, he addressed a public meeting at Ambala (in today's Haryana), from where he also sent a telegram to Sheikh Abdullah in which he conveyed his desire to proceed towards Jammu & Kashmir.

The next day, Sheikh Abdullah forwarded the telegram to the PM and the home minister in Delhi.

"My objective is to see for myself the present conditions in Jammu and also to contact people there. I am exploring the possibilities of creating conditions which may expedite a peaceful settlement and restoration of good feelings and understanding among all concerned," Mookerjee's telegram read. "After surveying situations in Jammu, I would welcome an opportunity to meet you as well."

On his way to Jammu and Kashmir, he went to Karnal from Ambala to address meetings at Shahabad and Nilokheri (both in present-day Haryana). On 9 May, he reached Panipat, from where his next stop was Jalandhar before he left for Amritsar.

In Amritsar, he again addressed meetings and press conferences on 10 May, and spent the night. He reached Pathankot on 11 May, and Sheikh Abdullah had replied to his telegram by then, describing his proposed visit as "inopportune."

Mookerjee reached Jammu and Kashmir from Pathankot. But as soon as he entered, he was arrested by the then Inspector General of Police, Jammu and Kashmir, in the presence of Maulana Masudi, then general secretary of Sheikh Abdullah's National Conference.

The Jana Sangh founder was taken straight to Jammu from where he was transferred to the Srinagar Central Jail. Soon after, he was moved to a small cottage at Nishat Bagh and kept under detention.

Mookerjee was detained in Srinagar for over a month. On 23 June 1953, he died while in detention in Srinagar under mysterious circumstances.

❑

13

Foreign Press, Indira and Emergency

On the night of 25 June, 1975, when Emergency was imposed in India by the then Prime Minister Indira Gandhi, the first casualty was the Indian Press. It was muzzled and free opinion was crushed through draconian censorship laws.

The second casualty was the foreign press. Many foreign correspondents were asked to leave the country. The first of the correspondents to be expelled was from The Washington Post; four days after the declaration of the state of Emergency. The correspondents of The Times (London), Newsweek, Far Eastern Economic Review and The Daily Telegraph left within next few days as they refused to sign an undertaking prepared by the Indira government which would commit them "to comply with the censorship guidelines and the instructions issued there under." The BBC had to close its New Delhi office in August, 1975.

Some members of the foreign press corps, however, managed to stay back in the country and wrote eye-opening accounts of the way Indira Gandhi acted as a dictator and Congress leaders and workers trampled upon democracy. These accounts are important as we do not get much information from the Indian newspapers and magazines about those days due to a severe clamp down on them.

These dispatches from some of the most reputed journalists across the world and their personal experiences revealed that Indira Gandhi was no less a dictator than Adolf Hitler. Evidence of this was provided by journalist Oriana Fallaci in an article dated 4 October, 1975 in The Australian.

"Mrs Gandhi had taken my arm and was relaxed and friendly after the tension of long hours of our interview. She asked about my job and what difficulties I encountered....but when we reached the outer door, she fell silent. An aged beggar lying on a heap of rags was asleep on the pavement. Besides him, a cow was evacuating its bowels soiling him with its excrement. I murmured, 'Things certainly do move a bit slowly in India.' I had barely uttered these words when five steely fingers gripped my arm and an icy voice retorted, 'What do you want me to do?' I am surrounded by a bunch of idiots. And Democracy!' I never reported the phrase because she had uttered it outside our interview. I am publishing it now because these words do much to explain the despotism with which she is ruling the country after the coup."

William Borders, like many others, drew an analogy in an article published in The New York

Times on 28 July, 1975. Talking about the excesses of the Indira government, Borders commented, "All this recalls the abuse of emergency powers under President Hindenburg in Weimar Germany that opened the way for Hitler." He went on to make another compelling observation: "...the two great names Mrs Gandhi dishonoured, that of her father Jawaharlal Nehru, and that of the founder of democratic India, Mohandas K. Gandhi...two men whose views would doubtless land them in jail today if they were still alive."

Eminent journalist Christopher Sweeney writes in one of his articles (The Guardian, 24 July, 1976), "At least twice my hotel room was broken into and searched. In Bombay, five hours after a meeting with JP Narayan, I returned to my hotel room to find the bottom torn out of a suitcase, drawers still open and clothes dumped in disorder." He goes on to add, "When I complained of the continued harassment by the government agents and asked Mr Haksar (the official spokesman of Ministry of Foreign Affairs) to explain why it had been necessary to organise breakings into my rooms, he replied that unless I left the country, as soon as possible, there would be a 'further prospect of physical inconvenience.'"

Le Monde (Paris) reported on 31 October, 1976, "Today the leader of the government is answerable to no one and the Indian Union's federal character has become blurred. The decision-making centres are the Prime Minister's Office, the police and the intelligence agencies."

The Times (London) reported on 14 October, 1976 that the Indian government had issued secret circulars to the Directorate of Audio-Visual Publicity (DAVP), the main arm of the government that released advertisements to the newspapers on behalf of government departments and ministries. These circulars specifically talked about banning the advertisements to publications that were not toeing the government line.

Many foreign newspapers also reported several deaths when people opposed compulsory sterilisation of men around the country and riots broke out; sterilisation was a favourite project of Indira's son Sanjay Gandhi, known to be one of the key figures behind the iron curtain. The issue has not been discussed much with most people not even being aware that such deaths had happened when police resorted to firing on common people opposing compulsory sterilisation.

The Congress' stand on Emergency has grave implications for the Indian democracy where a party refuses to be even apologetic about the past deeds of its leaders which were condemned worldwide and are considered to be the darkest time since India's independence.

❑

14

How BMS Replaced Left as Dominant Trade Union

Has the 'May Day' which has been celebrated in India as a 'Labour Day' on 1 May every year lost its relevance? Is it just a matter of time before India would officially replace '1 May' with 'Vishwakarma Day' to honour the contribution of workers in nation building?

Such questions are now raised increasingly on 1 May every year as Bharatiya Mazdoor Sangh (BMS), the largest trade union in India has shunned the celebration of 1 May as 'Labour Day' as a relic of the obsolete past when Communists dominated the trade union movement in India. One of the key symbols for BMS is celebration of Vishwakarma Day as National Labour Day to send a message across that the Left has lost its most traditional bastion to the nationalists.

How BMS displaced the Left

BMS was founded on 23 July, 1955—on the birth anniversary of Lokmanya Bal Gangadhar Tilak by a pracharak of RSS Dattopant Thengadi who is revered within the Sangh Parivar as one of the key ideologues. He is also credited for setting up organisations like Bharatiya Kisan Sangh, the largest farmers' organisation in the country and Swadeshi Jagaran Manch, an outfit that has batted for 'Atmanirbhar Bharat' since the early 1990s.

When BMS was set up, the labour movement in India was dominated by the Left and the Congress-backed trade unions. BMS took a different approach. Shunning the Marxist approach that believed in confrontation between the workers and the owners, it adopted a consensual approach based on 'nationalism'.

Thengadi played a key role in building the organisation brick by brick over the next few decades. Initially, the organisation focussed on the unorganised sector to create a toe-hold. According to BMS' official documents, "Shri Thengadiji and the local efforts of his then colleagues resulted in setting up of unions at several places. Of course, that looked insignificant in the broad canvas of the trade union field like tiny dots on a large map. Most of these unions were in the unorganised sector. With the increase in experience, slowly, BMS unions sprung up in important industries. In a few states, State Committees were formed."

The first watershed moment came in 1967 when 12 years after its formation, the first all India Conference was held in Delhi, in which the initial national executive was elected. At that time, the BMS had 541 affiliated unions and its total membership stood at 2,46,000. Thengadi was elected General Secretary and Ram Naresh was its first President.

In the post-1967 phase, it went on a rapid expansion mode and within 15 years became the second largest trade union in the country. "In 1984, after membership verification by the Central Government of all major Central Labour Organisations, declared BMS as the second largest Central Trade Union Organisation with 12,11,355 members," –BMS' official records.

The next important moment came when during 1996 it was declared the largest trade union in the country with a membership of 31,17,324 by the Union Ministry of Labour. The reckoning date of the above verification was 31 December 1989. In the subsequent verification held by the Government of India for the year 2002, BMS retained its position as the largest labour organisation in the country.

According to the BMS officials, "Of the 44 industries classified by the Ministry of Labour, Government of India for the purpose of membership verification, BMS has affiliated unions in all industries. BMS has membership of almost 1 crore in all states comprising more than 5000 affiliate unions."

Philosophy of BMS

According to BMS, "....(it) is productivity oriented non-political Central Trade Union Organisation. It... stands firmly for the principle of public accountability of each industry and consequent enunciation of public discipline. It tries to bring consumers as the third and the most important party to industrial relations. For the furtherance and realisation of its aims and objects, BMS applies all legitimate means consistent with the spirit of nationalism and patriotism."

Today BMS is significantly represented in most of the bipartite/tripartite labour and industrial committees/Boards constituted by the central government including Indian Labour Conference (ILC), Standing Labour Committee, Central Board for Workers Education, ESI, EPF, National Productivity Council, National Safety Council, Negotiation Committees of Public Sector Undertakings like BHEL, NTPC, NHPC, BEL, Coal, Industrial Committees of Jute, Textiles, Engineering, Chemical-Fertilisers, Sugar, Electricity, Transport and the consultative machinery of Government employees and various other Committees/Boards. BMS also leads the delegation of Indian workforce in the Conferences of International Labour Organisation (ILO).

Why Vishwakarma Jayanti and not May Day

Writing for the RSS backed English weekly Organiser BMS President CK Saji Narayan explained it in an article published in 2017 and republished in 2019, "Vishwakarma symbolises the paradigm shift in the present-day thought process. Work is considered as a Yajna. Indian Industrial relations are traditionally based on family-like relationship. BMS has accepted family as a model for industrial relations and put forward the great concept of 'Industrial family'. This is in contrast with the master-servant relationship of the

West or the class-enemy concept of the Communists. We have imbibed the slogans "Tyag-Tapasya-Balidan", "Work is worship", "Nationalise the Labour" etc. from the life of great personalities like Vishwakarma. To bring uniformity, Vishwakarma Jayanti is celebrated on 17 September every year. In many places, it is celebrated both on Bhadrapada Shukla Panchami as well as on Magha Shukla Thrayodasi. May Day, imported from the West, fails to motivate labour positively whereas Vishwakarma Jayanti can."

BMS on Measures for Workers During COVID-19

The BMS has been batting for the livelihoods of the workers during the time of COVID-19 pandemic since 2020. In its latest missive, the BMS general secretary Binoy Kumar Sinha wrote to Prime Minister Narendra Modi on 17 April to "take a quick call to stop (reverse) migration and provide work for these migrants in places of their stay."

He further added, "With One Nation One Ration card, it won't be tough for the government to identify such workers and help them out in crisis-like situation."

The BMS urged PM Modi "to kindly get into the dialogue with the state governments and direct them to ensure that (reverse) migration is halted for the upkeep of the faith of workers, life of industries and growth of the nation as per forecast."

❑

15

Thakur Ram Singh: An RSS Pracharak who Built a Movement to Rewrite Indian History

The debate on 'Rewriting of Indian history' has not simmered down ever since the BJP-led National Democratic Alliance (NDA) came to power in the 1990s. Attempts to rewrite history text books led to an ideological battle that continues to rage and is not expected to die down soon.

However, very few would know that the key force behind kicking off this debate and now carrying it forward is a low profiled organisation called Akhil Bharatiya Itihas Sankalan Yojana (ABISY). Even a lesser-known fact is that it was a non-descript pracharak of RSS, Thakur Ram Singh who built this organisation painstakingly resulting in a pan-India movement to challenge the Leftist historians and the textbooks written by them. ABISY has been able to take this ideological battle to its opponents' backyard, courtesy a strong and focussed organisation built under the leadership of Thakur Ram Singh within a short span of time.

Thakur Ram Singh was the founder president of Akhil Bharatiya Itihas Sankalan Yojana. The organisation was set up on 23 May 1994, in Delhi. He started building this organisation as soon as it was set up aided by several other colleagues which included senior RSS pracharak Moropant Pingle and noted historian Satish Chandra Mittal among others.

Immediately after setting up the organisation, he started a pan-India tour where he visited several university campuses, met historians and academicians from various fields associated directly or indirectly with history. This was the beginning of an exercise that focussed on building an extensive network of intellectuals who were dissatisfied with the popular discourse on India's history. The common ground for coming together was that India's history needs to be written from an Indian perspective and this had not been done after independence.

When Thakur Ram Singh took up this task, the Marxist interpretation of Indian history was dominating the academic discourse as well as textbooks in India. It was an uphill task to challenge it but he used the organisational skills which he had acquired while working within the RSS as pracharak for more than five decades to build a movement.

The first key debate kicked off by ABISY led by Thakur Ram Singh was that India should not adhere to the western framework of 'BC and AD' when it comes to looking at chronology. India's history dates back much older and it should devise its own time framework. Taking up similar issues, over a period of time ABISY set up around a dozen such projects challenging the Left and the western frameworks of Indian history. To name a few—History in Puranas, Debunking Aryan Invasion Theory, The science behind the Hindu calendar and its global expanse, History of pilgrimage centres of Bharat, Evidence-based history of war of independence in 1857, Vedic Saraswati River, Documenting tribal history, etc.

Thakur Ram Singh continued to work actively as President of ABISY till 2003. By that time, he had set up the units of the organisation at district level across the country. He had also framed the key objectives of the organisation that continue to guide its efforts.

Key objectives of ABISY

- Removing the distortions in Indian history.
- Reconstruct history by debunking the distortions on which Indian history is created.
- For this type of reconstruction, compilation of published and unpublished authentic material related to different disciplines of orientalism at district and village-level.
- Setting up a structure that facilitates writing history from the Indian point of view, at the district level, from the 'Mahabharata' period to the present. This should be done based on Hindu calendar.

- Establishing contacts with qualified individuals, institutions and organisations and motivating them.
- Organising programmes to generate respect, affection and interest in the heart of the common man for the specific achievements of Indian culture, orientalism and ancestors.
- Organising seminars, discussions and special lectures to encourage research related to Indian history, culture and archeology.

In 2003, Thakur Ram Singh stepped down from the post of president of ABISY due to old age. But he continued to guide it as a mentor. During the last few years of his life, he built a major research institute in Himachal Pradesh—Thakur Jagdev Chand Shodh Sansthan. According to ABISY's official website, Thakur Ram Singh's passion and commitment to the cause was such that at the age of 95, he had already planned to do certain more things for the next five years. One of his most famous quotes often remembered by his colleagues and who came in touch with him was, "We have to serve Bharat Mata, for first 50 years with black hair and then for next 50 years with white hair."

Early Life

Thakur Ram Singh was born on 16 February, 1915 in village Jhandvi, Tehsil Bhonraj, District Hamirpur, Himachal Pradesh. In 1942, he got an M.A. in History from Lahore University and became an RSS pracharak.

From 1949 to 1971 he worked in Assam expanding the organisational network. From 1971 to 1989 he worked as an RSS pracharak in Punjab. In 1990, he was given the responsibility to run Baba Saheb Apte Smarak Samiti, a predecessor of ABISY. Baba Saheb Apte was the first RSS pracharak. He was keenly interested to initiate the rewriting of history but during his life time an organisational structure for the same could not be set up. In 1973, Baba Saheb Apte Smarak Samiti was set up at Nagpur to do the early ground work in this field. Moropant Pingle, another senior RSS pracharak, also played a key role in taking forward the Samiti's work. Both Pingle and Thakur Ram Singh worked closely to make ABISY a key player in the battle for rewriting Indian history from the Indian perspective. The latter passed away on 6 September, 2010.

❑

16

How RSS Emerged from the first Ban

The Rashtriya Swayamsevak Sangh was banned for the first time since its inception in 1925 after Mahatma Gandhi's assassination on 30 January, 1948. The ban was imposed through a notification on 4 February 1948.

Though the ban was lifted on 12 July, 1949 after the government failed to find any evidence of the RSS' role in Mahatma's assassination, this ban played a significant role in shaping the RSS for its future role.

RSS and Politics

As soon as the ban was lifted, a discussion ensued within the organisation on RSS' role in independent India. A section of RSS functionaries wanted the RSS to be converted into a political party and get involved in electoral politics. The other section wanted RSS to stay away from active politics.

A middle path was found by the then Sarsanghchalak MS Golwalkar (popularly known as

Guruji). Dr Syama Prasad Mookerjee had resigned from Nehru's cabinet in protest against his policies. The former was thinking of setting up a new political party. He met Guruji, Balasaheb Deoras and Bhaurao Deoras in early 1951 at the home of Nagpur Sanghchalak Babasaheb Ghatate. It was decided to launch Bharatiya Jana Sangh after the discussions.

The RSS loaned out some of its pracharaks to help the cause of setting up a nationalist party while making it clear that the RSS would not be involved directly in any political activity. So, pracharaks like Deendayal Upadhyaya, Atal Bihari Vajpayee and Nanaji Deshmukh got associated with the Bharatiya Jana Sangh with Dr Mookerjee at the helm of affairs. Vajpayee later became Prime Minister of India. Many of the RSS functionaries loaned out to the newly formed outfit such as Lal Krishna Advani and Sunder Singh Bhandari among others played an important role in shaping up the present-day BJP which was a new avatar of the Bharatiya Jana Sangh after the latter was merged with the Janata Party in 1977. However, the Janata Party got disintegrated and BJP was set up in 1980.

The RSS stand till date remains the same that it would stay away from active politics and would be an ideological mentor only. Some of its Pracharaks are loaned out to the BJP whenever the latter seeks help. This template of coordination was evolved in as early as the 1950s.

Communication Strategy

Another key impact of this ban on the RSS was that it realised that it should help build mass media platforms where its voice is also carried. During the ban, the RSS was demonised by its detractors and there were very few voices who would publish the counter view. Following the lifting of the ban, the RSS encouraged its volunteers to run newspapers, periodicals, magazines in English and other India languages. In addition to strengthening its weekly 'Panchjanya' and 'Organiser', many other newspapers were started in years to come such as 'Tarun Bharat,' 'Swadesh' etc. Today, there are dozens of publications brought out by the RSS' ideological mentees which help the organisation to share its ideological perspective in almost every nook and corner of the nation.

The Art of Satyagraha

The third impact of the ban was that the RSS learnt the effectiveness of Satyagraha, a non-violent tool of protest first used by Mahatma Gandhi during the freedom struggle. More than 77,000 RSS volunteers courted arrest by launching the first Satyagraha after independence to protest this ban. This played a major role in compelling the government to lift the ban. Satyagraha was used by the RSS effectively during Emergency (1975–1977) again when it was banned for the second time.

Expansion and Galvanisation

The fourth impact was that the RSS made a

major effort to expand its reach and galvanise its organisation. The year 1952 saw the RSS inspiring its swayamsevaks to move into the field of education by setting up a model of Swadeshi education. There were detailed discussions between Guruji and Professor Rajendra Singh, Nanaji Deshmukh, Pandit Deendayal Upadhyaya and Bhaurao Deoras on this issue.

As a result, the first Saraswati Shishu Mandir came into existence under the leadership of Nanaji Deshmukh at Gorakhpur. All its teachers were graduates, who had retired from their pracharak life. Guruji laid the foundation stone of the building. Today, this movement has the largest number of schools in the country educating millions of students.

In 1952, the RSS also launched the Cow protection movement. The Akhil Bharatiya Pratinidhi Sabha (the highest decision-making body of the RSS) passed a resolution in Nagpur in September 1952 about banning cow slaughter across the country.

A massive nationwide campaign was launched. Guruji issued a statement: "The main objective of this signature collection is to submit a gigantic request containing crores of signatures to the President. This is an act of fiery patriotism. It is my request that each citizen of this country should rise above the differences of religion, sect, caste, party, etc. and participate in this sacred work." He wrote letters to political leaders, editors and religious heads individually. The signature campaign was formally launched by Sarkaryavah Bhaiyaji Dani and by Guruji in Mumbai. The RSS volunteers collected signatures from 94,459 villages and towns. Total count of signatures was one crore seventy-nine lakh eighty-nine thousand three hundred thirty-two (1,79,89,332)!"

Next day, on December 8, Guruji met the President to hand him over the signatures with an appeal to ban cow slaughter across the country.

One of the key impacts of the cow protection campaign was that it galvanised the RSS at an organisational level and increased its organisational reach significantly.

The RSS was now getting increasingly involved in the relief and rehabilitation efforts wherever a disaster or calamity struck in the country. This resulted in setting up of the 'Sewa Vibhag' (a wing for Social Services). Guided by the 'Sewa Vibhag', at present the RSS and organisations inspired by it are running around two lakh social welfare projects across the country.

(The above information has been sourced from 'Shri Guruji Samagra' (Vol.1 to10), 'The Saffron Surge: Untold Story of RSS Leadership' and RSS archives)

❑

17

Vanvasi Kalyan Ashram: How the RSS, a Congress Stalwart and a Gandhian Crystallised the Idea

India's largest tribal welfare organisation, the Akhil Bharatiya Vanvasi Kalyan Ashram (ABVKA) was founded on 26 December, 1952. The organisation, which is backed by RSS and has been at the forefront of anti-conversion campaign, can interestingly trace back its roots to not only the second RSS Sarsanghalak MS Golwalkar but also to Congress stalwart Pandit Ravi Shankar Shukla and a Gandhian—Thakkar Bappa.

It all began immediately after India attained independence. Pandit Ravi Shankar Shukla, a senior Congress leader and Chief Minister of Madhya Pradesh at that time went on a tour of the tribal areas. He was welcomed at all the places by local population except in Jashpur (now in Jharkhand), an area which had heavy population of tribals. In Jashpur, Shukla was shown black flags and asked to go back by some protesters. When he came back and enquired, it turned out that some of the Christian missionaries who were involved in conversion of tribals to Christianity in this area had a hand in it. Concerned over the conversion activities, he consulted Gandhian leader Thakkar Bappa, who had experience of extensively working in the tribal areas. The latter suggested the Chief Minister to set up a social welfare department specifically for the backward communities in that area. In 1948, this department was set up and Pandurang Govind Vanikar, a close associate of Bappa, became its first director.

It was quite challenging to work in Jashpur at that time. It was a remote and extremely backward area and on top of that there was strong resistance from well entrenched Christian missionaries also. Vanikar needed a trusted aide and he asked Ramakant Keshav Deshpande, an RSS swayamsevak (volunteer) to come and join him. Deshpande was practicing law in Ramtek (at present in Maharashtra). He left his practice and joined the department where he was appointed as the 'Area Organiser' for Jashpur region.

Deshpande reached Jashpur in early 1948 and toured the area extensively. Initially the state government had sanctioned budget for only 8 schools but Deshpande not only got the budget for 100 schools but within a year opened them also.

A Gandhian, Bappa was so impressed with this that he himself visited some of these schools at the age of 80 in 1949 and gave a special award of Rs 250 to Deshpande. In January1951, Bappa passed away and Deshpande realised that he would not be able to do much for tribals within the administrative set up. He had also realised while working in the area that a nationalist social organisation needs to be set up to meet the challenge of conversions and work for all round development of the tribals.

Deshpande met the second RSS Sarsanghchalak Guruji and discussed the issue with him. Guruji drafted an experienced, highly committed and soft-spoken RSS pracharak (full-time worker) Moreshwar Haribhau Ketkar to assist Deshpande. These developments finally culminated in the setting up of ABVKA commonly known as Vanvasi Kalyan Ashram at Jashpur on 26 December, 1952. The first project started by the organisation had only 13 tribal children who were enrolled to be educated, with hostel facilities.

At present, the organisation runs more than 20,000 projects covering almost every aspect related to the welfare of the tribals. Its work has been expanded to 323 districts of the country. It has a footprint in more than 52,000 villages. It has 14000 village level committees. The organisation has 1,200 full-time workers, 70 per cent of them are tribals. The full-time workers also include 300 women.

During COVID-19, the organisation was at the forefront of providing relief in tribal areas. According to an official communiqué of the organisation, its 9000 volunteers reached out to 38,000 tribal families in 1900 villages across 21 states and Union Territories including Andaman and Nicobar Islands covering 101 Scheduled tribes. In addition to providing sanitisers, masks, dry rations etc, it also helped the tribal workers and students stuck in other cities to get back to their homes. It ran 421 centres where tribal women made more than 33000 masks.

Deshpande continued to guide the organisation till he passed away in 1995. The mantle of the president of Akhil Bharatiya Vanvas Kalyan Ashram (ABVKA) was taken over by Jagdev Ram Oraon. A local resident, he had joined the organisation as a teacher in 1968 and worked relentlessly for the organisation as a full timer. Under his leadership ABVKA made rapid strides and became more vocal in the public discourse. It came out with a detailed vision document on tribals and expanded its outreach across the country. Oraon passed away in July 2020 at the age of 72. Ramchandra Kharadi was appointed as the president of ABVKA in October 2020. He is the third president of the organisation since its inception.

❑

18

What Foreign Press had to say about the Role of RSS during Emergency?

As the Indira Gandhi government imposed Emergency in India at midnight of June 25-26, 1975, the role of foreign press became important as most of the Indian newspapers and magazines had become victims of the ruthless censorship for the next 19 months.

It was left to a large extent to the foreign press to highlight the pro-democracy movement which stood against the draconian measures taken by Indira Gandhi's government. Interestingly, the dispatches from foreign journalists posted in Delhi repeatedly highlighted the role played by Rashtriya Swayam sevak Sangh (RSS) in the movement to restore democracy.

The Economist wrote on January 24 1976 in an article titled, 'Yes there is an Underground', "In formal terms the underground is an alliance of four opposition parties: the Jana Sangh, the Socialist Party, the breakaway fraction of the Congress Party and

Lok Dal. But the shock troops of the movement come largely from the Jana Sangh and its banned affiliate, the RSS, which claim a combined membership of 10million (of whom 80,000 including 6,000 full-time party workers are in prison)."

It further mentioned specifically that two of the top four leaders that were running the Underground movement were from RSS and Jana Sangh. They were—Dattopant Thengadi, a senior RSS pracharak and Dr Subramaniam Swamy from BJS. "The day-to-day activities of the movement are directed by a four-man committee which meets three times a week sometimes in Delhi, sometimes in Bombay (now Mumbai), Madras (now Chennai), or Ahmedabad and sometimes on a train in between the cities. The top man on the committee is Ravindra Verma, a former Congress Member of Parliament from Kerala who is now a member of the opposition Congress. The other three are DP Thengadi, a trade union leader, SM Joshi a former socialist MP and Subramanyam Swamy, a Jana Sangh member of the upper house."

In another dispatch, The Economist wrote: "The underground campaign against Mrs Gandhi claims to be the only non-left wing revolutionary force in the world disavowing both bloodshed and class struggle. Indeed, it might even be called right wing since it is dominated by Jana Sangh and its banned cultural affiliate the RSS but its platform at the moment has only one non-ideological plank—to bring back democracy to India."

It further added, "The truth of this operation consists of tens of thousands of cadres who are organised down to the village level into 4 man-cells. Most of them are RSS regulars.... the other opposition parties which started out as partners in the underground have effectively abandoned the field to the Jan Sangh and RSS. The function of the RSS cadre network.... is mainly to spread the anti-Gandhi word. Once the ground is prepared and political consciousness raised, so the leaders are ready, any spark can set off the revolutionary Prairie fire."

Bursting the propaganda of Indira Gandhi's government against the RSS, J. Anthony Lukas wrote in an article titled 'India is as Indira Does' in The New York Times Magazine on April 4, 1976, "The Rashtriya Swayamsevak Sangh, commonly known as the RSS are a tightly disciplined band of volunteers between the ages of 12 and 21, but they can hardly be called "troops". Pictures of material seized from the RSS offices after the Emergency primarily show long wooden staves and wooden swords. I asked Om Mehta, a Minister of State in the Home Ministry, about this and he replied vaguely. 'There were some metal swords too'. Even with some metal swords, I asked, how could boys with staves pose much of a threat to a superbly equipped army of about one million men, the Border Security Force of about 85,000, the Central Reserve Police of about 57,000 and some 755,000 state policemen. 'Well,' Mehta said, 'there were undoubtedly some rifles'. Did you seize any? I asked. 'No,' he said. 'But they probably kept them at home. Do not underestimate these people's capacity for mischief.'"

Many RSS workers had gone underground and crossed over the border to Nepal to evade arrest in India. The Guardian wrote in an article titled, 'The Empress Reigns Supreme' (2 August, 1976), "Reports from Kathmandu say that the Nepalese government has rejected appeals from the Indian police to arrest and intern members of the Indian underground."

It added, "A source close to the Nepalese embassy said that Kathmandu will never hand over to the Indian government members of the RSS...banned by the Gandhi regime shortly after the promulgation of the Emergency...."

Quoting the then Indian Home Minister about his views on the RSS, The Guardian said in same article, "The RSS continues to be active all over India," Brahmananda Reddy, the Indian Home Minister said recently... "It has even extended its tentacles to far off Kerala in the South."

Commenting on the role of Communists, the same article said, "...Pro-CPI (Communist Party of India) journals in India are being given some latitude by the censors because the party is in favour of even stronger measures to suppress the non-communist opposition."

The New York Times reported on 28 October, 1976 in an article titled, 'Senator Wheeldon (Western Australia) in Australian Parliament', "The only political parties which are supporting Congress Party of the government in the actions that it is taking are the Communist Party of India, the pro-Moscow Communist party and the Moslem League."

❑

19

Hindu Samrajya Divas: Why and how RSS is Reviving a Forgotten Chapter of History?

The Rashtriya Swayamsevak Sangh celebrates 'Hindu Samrajya Diwas', (one of the six festivals it celebrates officially at the organisational level) every year. The five other festivals that the RSS celebrates at its daily shakhas once in a year are—Vijayadashmi, Makar Sankranti, Varsh Pratipada Mahotsav, Gurupurnima and Rakshabandhan Mahotsav.

This particular festival—'Hindu Samrajya Divas' marks the coronation of Chatrapati Shivaji in 1674 on Jyeshtha Shukla Trayodashi, according to Hindu calendar. Though, according to Gregorian calendar, Shivaji's coronation was done on June 6, 1674. The RSS goes by the Hindu calendar and hence the celebrations are carried out on more than 60,000 RSS Shakhas and by more than three dozen organisations backed by the Sangh. The RSS believes that with coronation, a 'Hindu Samrajya (Kingdom)' came into existence and hence the reason to celebrate and remember it.

Indicating how important it is to remember the 'Swaraj' set up by Shivaji, Anil Madhav Dave, a former RSS functionary, who held the portfolio of Environment ministry in 2016-17 published an exhaustive book 'Shivaji and Suraj: 22 original edicts on the art of leadership' in 2017. The RSS Sarsanghchalak Mohan Bhagwat and Prime Minister Narendra Modi both wrote detailed 'Introduction' and 'Preface' for the book. (Dave suddenly passed away in May 2017.)

Bhagwat wrote in the 'Introduction' for this book, "The Kingdom and administration established by Shivaji Maharaj in the 17th century remains relevant, ideal and topic of research for almost all classes and sections of the populace of the country even today."

Prime Minister Modi wrote in the 'Preface' of the book, "...Shivaji is relevant to us even in this age. Today, when the nation yearns for good governance, it will be relevant to recall thatcenturies ago, the foundation of Shivaji's Kingdom was laid on the basis of this very principle of good governance."

Why Did the RSS Choose these Six Festivals?

The philosophy behind this move has been explained in a publication titled, 'Sangh Utsav' (Suruchi Prakashan) based on the writings and speeches of MS Golwalkar, the second Sarsanghchalak of the RSS and Bala Saheb Deoras, the third Sarsanghchalak of RSS. It says, "The RSS has chosen these festivals as they synergise with its objectives and name. One must understand here that Sangh has not created any new festival. But these festivals are of national importance and the Hindu society has been celebrating them since time immemorial."

There is one exception to this: 'Hindu Samrajya Divas', which was not celebrated at national level till the RSS included it in its list. And 'Sangh Utsav', accepting this fact, adds, "Hindu Samrajya Divas is a festival that inspires an awakening in the society. That is why Sangh has included it in the list of other traditional festivals."

The reason for celebrating these festivals is further explained, "Memories of the great personalities who made sacrifices are associated with these festivals. So we (the RSS swayamsevaks), awaken the society through these festivals."

More importantly, the celebrations of these festivals help the RSS to expand its base. The festivals are generally celebrated at the Shakha level. "Once a Shakha decides to celebrate the festival, this helps to showcase the RSS' ideology and work, to the local community. It helps to bring the local community closer to the Sangh. Thus, these festivals play an important role in creating a conducive environment for the expansion of the RSS."

Hindu Samrajya Divas

This festival is different from the rest of the festivals celebrated by the RSS. "While the rest of the festivals celebrated by the RSS are also celebrated by the common people outside RSS also, it is the only festival which has generally not been celebrated in the society at mass level. In fact, many people even don't know that a historical event took place, which deserves to be celebrated." ('Sangh Utsav').

The RSS celebrated this festival as it believes that along with this coronation, a Hindu Kingdom came into existence officially as Shivaji himself announced that day, "Hindu self rule should be established, that is the will of the God." He also said, "This kingdom does not belong to Shivaji but to the dharma."

According to 'Sangh Utsav', "The Hindus were at the receiving end when this momentous event happened and it electrified the Hindu consciousness across the country. It was the time when Hindus could not even think of being rulers. The morale of Hindus was so low that they could not think of reaching up to that level and they had accepted that only Muslims can become rulers and Hindus can only serve them. In such a desperate situation, Shivaji's act of setting up a Hindu Kingdom boosted the morale of the Hindus immensely. So, if we have to move on our path rightly, it is imminent to remember great men like Shivaji who created history."

This festival is generally celebrated at the RSS Shakha by worshipping portraits of Shivaji and his master (Guru) Samarth Ramdas. The famous letter written by Shivaji to Rajput King Jai Singh is also read on this occasion. The letter calls upon the Rajput warrior not to shed the blood of Hindus for Mughals and exhorts him to join Shivaji for the greater cause.

On this occasion, anecdotal tales of Shivaji's valour are shared by the senior Sangh functionaries in the form of intellectual discourses with swayamsevaks.

Tributes are also offered to Shivaji's mother Jijabai on this occasion. In fact, Jijabai, along with Shivaji, remains one of the most revered figures in Sangh Parivar for the way she motivated her son to fight back the Mughals and set up Dharma Rajya, which may be broadly translated as the 'Rule of Righteousness.'

As part of the celebrations, swayamsevaks also recite patriotic songs especially penned for the festival by many writers.

❑

20

Nanaji Deshmukh: A Multi-dimensional Social Reformer

It is not very common in Indian politics that a politician quits public life at the peak of his career, takes up social service and then ends up getting the Bharat Ratna, the country's highest civilian award. But that is what Nanaji Deshmukh exactly did.

"When the Janata Party government was formed in 1977, Nanaji Deshmukh was requested to join the government as a minister but he did not do so. He followed JP (Jaiprakash Narayan) and preferred to devote himself towards rural development and making our villages self-reliant, free from poverty," Prime Minister Narendra Modi had said while inaugurating the birth centenary celebrations of Nanaji a few years ago.

After quitting politics in 1980, Nanaji, through the Deendayal Research Institute (DRI), set up alternative rural development models based on traditional knowledge in the remote areas of Gonda and Chitrakoot in Uttar Pradesh and Madhya Pradesh respectively. Some were established in Maharashtra's Beed too.

In 2019, he was awarded the 'Bharat Ratna' posthumously.

His contributions in the field of rural development and social transformation were carried forward by the DRI, which has now expanded its work to many more states.

Let us take a look at Nanaji's journey in the RSS, friendship with Deendayal Upadhyaya, his role during the Emergency and fight against corruption.

Meeting Deendayal Upadhyaya

Born on 11 October 1916, at Kadoli, a small town in Maharashtra, Chandikadas Amritrao Deshmukh (affectionately called Nanaji) worked as a vegetable seller to pay for his early education. Through hard work and dedication, he later graduated from the prestigious Birla Institute of Technology and Science in Pilani, Rajasthan.

His family was in touch with Dr KB Hedgewar, founder of the RSS. Inspired by freedom fighter Lokmanya Tilak and his thoughts on nationalism, Nanaji joined the RSS as a pracharak (full-time worker) around 1940.

As a pracharak, he was first sent to Uttar Pradesh and it was in Agra that he met Deendayal Upadhyaya, who later became one of the founders of the Bharatiye

Janasangh (BJS), the prodectssor of BJP.

Nanaji and Upadhyaya worked closely for nearly three decades. The rapport between the two was so strong that after Upadhyaya's death in February 1968, Nanaji founded the DRI in his friend's memory.

From Agra, Nanaji went to Gorakhpur as a pracharak to expand organisational work in eastern Uttar Pradesh. In a span of three years, over 250 RSS shakhas were established in the region.

He also played a key role in establishing India's first Saraswati Shishu Mandir School at Gorakhpur in 1952. Today, there are more than 20,000 such schools running across the country and catering to over three million students.

In 1947, the RSS decided to launch two journals 'Rashtra Dharma' and 'Panchjanya' as well as a daily named 'Swadesh'. Atal Bihari Vajpayee was appointed as the editor, Upadhyaya the 'margdharshak' (mentor), and Nanaji was appointed as the managing director.

Expert at stitching alliances

Nanaji played a crucial role in setting up a strong base for the BJS in Uttar Pradesh. By 1957, the party had a presence in every district of the state, with Nanaji as the organising secretary of its state unit. He later also worked as the party's treasurer.

As a politician, he was known for his expertise in stitching alliances. In 1967, the first non-Congress government in Uttar Pradesh came to power through an alliance which was put together by socialist leader Ram Manohar Lohia and Nanaji.

His organisational skills were best displayed during the Emergency in 1975-76. He led the underground movement against Prime Minister Indira Gandhi and her regime for restoration of democracy.

Prior to that, he also played an important role in the expansion of the 'JP movement' that was spearheaded by veteran freedom fighter Jaiprakash Narayan against corruption in the Congress regime.

JP and Nanaji enjoyed such a close bond that the latter named a flagship rural transformation project of DRI in Gonda after the names of both Narayan and his wife Prabhavati Devi. It was called 'JaiPrabha Gram'.

In 1977, he was one of the key architects of the opposition alliance that finally took the shape of Janata Party. Nanaji contested elections for the first time and won from Balrampur (Uttar Pradesh) in 1977.

He was later offered a ministerial post by Prime Minister Morarji Desai but he politely refused. Nanaji announced his retirement from politics in 1980, after the Janata Party split and the BJP was formed.

The rest of his life was devoted to the cause of rural transformation through two key concepts—'Gramodaya' (rise of the village) and 'Swawalamban' (self-reliance).

He also established India's first rural university, Chitrakoot Gramodaya Vishwavidyalaya, in Chitrakoot.

In recognition of his services to the nation, he was nominated as a member of the Rajya Sabha in 1999. He was also awarded Padma Vibhushan in 1999. Nanaji passed away on 27 February 2010 in Chitrakoot.

S. Gurumurthy, another RSS stalwart, who had extensively interacted with Nanaji, had written in an article in The Indian Express (3 March 2010), "He (Nanaji) once told me that when he was a child, he had nothing to eat for many days. But that did not turn him into a Naxalite. But his introduction to the RSS at the right age, and association with the right people had turned him into a great nationalist who lived for his motherland's glory and nothing else."

❑

21

Who killed Deendayal Upadhyaya?

On the 55th birth anniversary of Deendayal Upadhyaya in 1971, Nanaji Deshmukh, his colleague in the Rashtriya Swayamsevak Sangh (RSS) for nearly three decades, had lamented how Upadhyaya's death remained a mystery even after three years.

On 11 February 1968, Upadhyaya, the then president of Bharatiya Janasangh (BJS) was found dead under mysterious circumstances at the Mughalsarai railway station near Varanasi in Uttar Pradesh.

"Today we are celebrating the 55th birth anniversary of Pandit Deendayal Upadhyaya but there are tears in our eyes," Deshmukh said, addressing a gathering in New Delhi in 1971. "Panditji was not only murdered, but nothing could even be discovered about his murderers. Neither the Central Bureau of Investigation (CBI) nor the Chandrachud Inquiry Commission could tell why and who murdered Deendayalji. It seems the government (then headed by Prime Minister Indira Gandhi), out of fear that the political results of this would be bad, did not want the murderers and their accomplices to be caught."

In 1968, in his friend's memory, Deshmukh established the Deendayal Research Institute (DRI) that still does pioneering work in the field of transformation of rural India. It was a subject close to Upadhyaya's heart as he is also credited with propounding the concept of 'Integral Humanism', which is the official ideology of the present-day BJP and holds rural transformation as the key to building a stronger India.

But some four decades since that speech by Deshmukh, the question—Who killed Deendayal Upadhyaya?—remains unanswered.

A mysterious death

After Upadhyaya's body was found on the railway tracks at Mughalsarai station, which was renamed as Deen Dayal Upadhyaya railway station in 2018, the then central government had handed over the inquiry to the CBI.

At that time, the CBI director was John Lobo, who had a reputation of being an upright and honest officer. As soon as the inquiry was handed over to the CBI, Lobo went to Mughalsarai with his team. But before he could complete his work, he was called back. The development led to suspicion that the direction of the investigation was being changed.

The CBI in its inquiry report concluded that the murder was an ordinary crime. According to the

CBI report, two petty thieves had murdered Pandit Deendayal Upadhyaya and their motive was theft.

A special sessions court gave its verdict on the basis of this CBI report, creating a stir with the statement that "the real truth still has to be found." The verdict came on 9 June, 1969.

The judge's remarks in court sparked a furore, prompting the then Indira Gandhi government to constitute an inquiry commission.

The commission, appointed on 23 October 1969, five months after the court verdict, was headed by Justice YV Chandrachud.

The commission made some interesting observations.

Stranger than Fiction: Commission

The Chandrachud Commission did note that Upadhyaya was murdered under mysterious circumstances.

"What happened in Mughalsarai, in parts, is stranger than fiction. Several people behaved abnormally to create suspicions. Whatever they did in such comparative circumstances is against the ordinary human behaviour that is hoped for. In the same way, some events in Mughalsarai are knitted to some abnormal fabrication," the commission said in its report. "When ordinary hopes are falsified regarding men and events, then suspicions arise. In this matter there is no end to such suspicious circumstances. All this builds a nebulousness that attempts to cover up the actual affair."

The day he was murdered, Upadhyaya was travelling on the Lucknow-Sealdah Express, headed to Patna from Lucknow. Half the bogey in which he was travelling was part of the third class and the other half was the first class. In Railway parlance, it was an FCT bogie.

Upadhyaya was travelling first class

There were three coupes in the bogie that belonged to the first class—A, B and C. There were four berths in A, two in B and four in C.

Upadhyaya's berth was in Coupe A, which he had changed for the Coupe B. He was the sole passenger in it. He had exchanged his berth with legislative council member Gauri Shanker Rai. The other passenger in Coupe A was MP Singh, a government officer.

Major SM Sharma had a reservation for Coupe C, but he did not travel in that coupe and instead travelled in the train service coach.

"The warp and weft of the sequence of events prima facie is no less than some terrifying James Bond movie. Major SM Sharma's name was written wrongly, not once, but twice, to the extent that even his ticket number was written wrongly," the commission said in its report. "Although his marriage had taken place only a few days earlier, even then he had shifted his date of travel beforehand; the conflicting testimonies given by

MP Singh's travelling companions and the conductor, BD Kamal; the changing of the state of the body, the discovery of a legitimate ticket in the pocket of the deceased, through which he could be identified easily; despite the attempt to settle his body in a makeshift manner, the discovery of a bottle of phenyl in the compartment; the strangeness of the injuries and many other such questions reflect an aberrance. The interesting thing is that at every step the involvement of some Railway employee or the other is found."

The RSS Pracharak who headed the Jana Sangh

Deendayal Upadhyaya was born on 25 September, 1916, in the village of Nagla Chandrabhan in UP's Mathura district. His mother Rampyari was a religious-minded lady and his father Bhagwati Prasad, was an assistant station master at Jalesar.

In 1937, he completed his B.A. from the Sanatan Dharma College in Kanpur. His friend Balwant Mahashabde played an instrumental role in convincing him to join the RSS in 1937. A few years later, he became an RSS pracharak.

Upadhyaya established the publishing house, 'Rashtra Dharma Prakashan', in Lucknow and launched the monthly magazine, 'Rashtra Dharma'. He later launched the weekly 'Panchjanya' and the daily 'Swadesh'.

He is known to have burnt all his educational certificates after becoming an RSS pracharak so that he could serve the organisation and the cause single-mindedly. In December 1967, he was elected as the president of BJS.

(All the information used in this report has been sourced from 'Complete Works of Deendayal Upadhyaya', Vol.1-15, Prabhat Prakashan).

❑

22

Nehru, J.P., Ambedkar: Pranab Mukherjee was not First Non-Sangh Leader to Connect with RSS

Former President and Congress stalwart Pranab Mukherjee's visit to an RSS training camp had created quite a flutter in 2018. The reason: For most of his political career, Mukherjee had been a senior leader of the Congress, which is perceived to be anti-Sangh by most political pundits.

And this perception is not without reason as the Congress has banned the RSS thrice—in 1948, in 1975 and in 1992.

However, Pranab Mukherjee's visit to the RSS event in Nagpur on 7 June 2018 was not an exception. Many leaders cutting across political lines, including Congress stalwarts, have been associated with the RSS or have been in touch with it since its inception in 1925.

In fact, almost eight-and-a-half decades before Mukherjee's visit, Mahatma Gandhi had visited an RSS training camp at Wardha in 1934. On 16 September 1947, while addressing RSS workers in one of his speeches in Delhi, Mahatma recalled, "I visited the RSS camp years ago, when the founder, Shri (KB) Hedgewar, was alive. I was very much impressed by your discipline, the complete absence of untouchability, and the rigorous simplicity. Since then, the Sangh has grown. I am convinced that any organisation, which is inspired by the high ideal of service and self-sacrifice, is bound to grow in strength."

Dr Bhimrao Ambedkar visited an RSS training camp—the Sangh Shiksha Varga—at Pune in 1939. When Dr Ambedkar asked Dr Hedgewar whether there were any untouchables in the camp, the RSS founder replied that there were neither touchables nor untouchables, but only Hindus there.

Ambedkar said, "I am surprised to find the swayamsevaks moving about in absolute equality and brotherhood without even caring to know the caste of the others."

In the 1950s, Ambedkar and RSS pracharak Dattopant Thengadi worked together closely and were constantly in touch.

RSS 'has historic role to play'

Prime Minister Jawaharlal Nehru, who was initially quite critical of the RSS, invited the organisation to participate in the Republic Day parade of 1963. The invitation was extended in recognition of the stellar work done by RSS volunteers during the 1962 India-China war. A 3,000-strong contingent of RSS volunteers participated in the Republic Day parade that year.

In 1965, when Pakistan attacked India, the then Prime Minister Lal Bahadur Shastri invited the second Sarsanghchalak of the RSS, MS Golwalkar, for an all-party consultative meeting, though the RSS was a non-political entity.

Golwalkar was travelling through Maharashtra and was stationed in Sangli for organisational work when he received this message. He immediately flew to New Delhi to attend the meeting.

Socialist and revolutionary leader Jaiprakash Narayan visited an RSS training camp in Patna on 3 November 1977, where he said in his speech: "Sangh (RSS) is a revolutionary organisation and right now there is no other organisation in the country which comes even close to it... (it) alone has the capacity to transform society, end casteism and wipe the tears from the eyes of the poor. Its very name is 'rashtriya', that is national. I am not saying this to flatter you. I believe you have a historic role to play.... I have great expectations from this revolutionary organisation which has taken up the challenge of creating a new India."

Earlier, in the 1960s, a host of leaders visited and appreciated the Vivekananda Rock Memorial at Kanyakumari that was set up under the guidance of RSS pracharak and former sarkaryavah Eknath Ranade.

The then President VV Giri inaugurated the celebrations after the memorial was completed. The then Prime Minister Indira Gandhi visited it after a fortnight of its inauguration. She addressed a meeting of the memorial organising committee, whose secretary was Ranade. The latter also presented a report after the PM's address.

Prime Minister Indira Gandhi commented during her visit, "It is a moving experience to come to Kanyakumari and see how the faith of thousands in Swami Vivekananda's message has made possible this memorial. May it inspire all who visit it and give them the courage to live up to Swamiji's great and timeless teachings."

In the 1980s, an organisation called the 'Virat Hindu Samaj' was set up to launch an anti-conversion campaign after many Dalits converted to Islam in Tamil Nadu's Meenakshipuram. Well-known Congress leader Dr Karan Singh, a former member of the Indira Gandhi cabinet, was the president of this organisation, and the general secretary's post was held by Ashok Singhal, who was the prant pracharak of the RSS in Delhi.

This platform organised a massive conference of Hindus in New Delhi that was attended by around five lakh people. In addition, hundreds of small and big conferences were organised throughout the country. Singhal later played a stellar role in the Ram Janmabhoomi movement launched by the VHP.

(Information used in this report has been sourced from the book, 'The Saffron Surge: Untold Story of RSS Leadership' and RSS archives)

❑

23

Facts about RSS Founder you did not Know

The birth anniversary of the founder of RSS Dr Keshav Baliram Hedgewar falls on the first day of the Hindu New Year, which is also known as 'Varsha Pratipada'.

The RSS does not count birth dates of its founder by the Gregorian calendar and goes by the Hindu calendar, and, therefore, there could be a different date in the Gregorian calendar for Hedgewar's anniversary who was born in 1889 and passed away in 1940.

Meanwhile, based on the information available at the RSS archives, here are some interesting facts that bust several myths about Hedgewar.

Dr Hedgewar lost his parents at the age of 13.

Many critics of the RSS have linked its initial years with domination of Maharashtra Brahmins. But, the RSS founder's family originally hailed from Kandkurti village in Telangana region.

Near the village is the sacred confluence of

Godavari, Vanjra and Haridra rivers. This confluence finds mention in several Indian sacred texts.

The place also witnessed a confluence of three robust Indian languages—Kannada, Telugu and Marathi. At one time, the place was a hub of scholars. But to look out for better opportunities, many Brahmin families left Telangana region.

Many of them settled down in Nagpur as the Bhonsle Rulers were known to be patrons of Vedic learning. Among them was Narhari Shastri, whose great grandson was Baliram Pant Hedgewar.

Baliram along with his wife Revatibai had six children—three sons, Mahadev, Seetaram and Keshav (who later became Dr KB Hedgewar), and three daughters, Saroo, Rajoo and Rangoo.

Keshav was the fifth child. At the age of 13, Keshav lost both his parents to plague and faced severe economic hardships while studying in school. He, literally, had to raise himself.

Was active in Congress

Around 1919, Hedgewar became very active in the Indian National Congress. He attended the Amritsar Session of Congress in 1919.

He was an active member of 'Rashtriya Mandal', a group formed by the followers of Lokmanya Bal Gangadhar Tilak in Nagpur Congress. He worked actively to promote a Hindi weekly 'Sankalpa'.

To inspire the youth through the lives of national heroes of India, he founded the 'Rashtriya Utsav Mandal'.

Looked after setting up corps of 1,500 volunteers

In January 1920, Dr LV Paranjpe started the Bharat Swayamsevak Mandal. Hedgewar was an active member of the mandal and worked closely with Dr Paranjpe.

In July 1920, efforts began to set up a corps of around 1,000–1,500 volunteers for the Congress session. Hedgewar was at the forefront of organising this corps. However, even as these efforts were going on by enthusiastic supporters of Lokmanya Tilak, tragedy struck.

Tilak passed away on the night of 31 July 1920. After Tilak's demise, Dr BS Moonje and Hedgewar went to Pondicherry (now Puducherry). Both of them met philosopher-poet Aurobindo Ghose and urged him to come and preside over the Congress session, but he refused.

The Congress session took place in December 1920. It was attended by over 3,000 members of the Reception Committee, nearly 15,000 delegates and thousands of common people. Dr Paranjpe and Hedgewar were in-charge of lodging and food for the delegates.

Jailed for 'sedition'

In May 1921, Hedgewar was arrested on charges of 'sedition' for his "objectionable" speeches at Katol and Bharatwada in Maharashtra region and imprisoned by a British judge for one year.

He was released in July 1922 from Ajani jail and the same evening, a public reception was organised in which then senior Congress leaders Motilal Nehru (father of India's first Prime Minister Jawaharlal Nehru), and Hakim Ajmal Khan also addressed the gathering.

When he decided to set up an outfit for Hindus

Hedgewar was appointed a joint secretary of the Provincial Congress in 1922. He was also part of the Hindusthani Seva Dal, a Congress wing of volunteers.

The Seva Dal was set up by Dr NS Hardikar of Hubli whom Hedgewar had known from his student days. The communal riots that broke out in 1923 in the wake of the Khilafat Movement proved to be a tipping point.

Hedgewar felt that the Congress leadership failed to address the concern of Hindus and so it was the time to set up an organisation to unite Hindus nationwide.

Sent to Kolkata to train for revolutionary work

Hedgewar was sent to study in the National Medical College in Calcutta (now Kolkata) by the

Nagpur group of revolutionaries in the middle of 1910.

He received financial help from Dajisaheb Buti, a member of the Nagpur group of revolutionaries. He was sent to Calcutta primarily to receive training for revolutionary work under the supervision of Pulin Bihari Das, a top leader of the revolutionary group Anushilan Samiti.

Supplied arms as member of a revolutionary group

As a member of the Anushilan Samiti, one of the prime tasks of Hedgewar was to ensure distribution of underground literature and arms to other parts of the country.

His friends acted as couriers and whenever he himself went to Nagpur, he would take revolvers for revolutionaries there. His code name among the revolutionaries was 'Koken.'

After completing his five-year medicine course, Hedgewar returned to Nagpur in early 1916. He got a lucrative job offer in Bangkok after clearing the final examination but he refused to take it up.

Instead, he set up a revolutionary group called 'Kranti Dal' with the help of Bhauji Karve, a nationalist from Nagpur.

One of his biggest influencers

One of the major influences on Hedgewar in his formative years was of Dr SK Malik, MS, MD from

Edinburgh and principal of the National Medical College.

Dr Malik had stayed and practised abroad for several years and yet his lifestyle did not bear any cultural influence of the West. He preferred to speak in his mother tongue everywhere and used English only while teaching in the college.

Hedgewar often used to quote Dr Malik's example whenever someone flaunted use of English against the use of Indian languages.

His friends in Kolkata

Though Hedgewar had developed close affinity with all the important nationalists of Bengal, the two leaders who were closest to him were Shamsundar Chakravarti and Moulvi Liaquat Hussain.

Chakravarti had returned to Calcutta (now Kolkata) in 1910 after a period of solitary confinement in Burma (now Myanmar). He regularly wrote fierce anti-British articles for 'Prativasi', 'Sandhya', 'Vande Mataram' and many other periodicals.

He was so poor that he would often have only a single 'dhoti' and would walk on the streets of Calcutta barefoot.

Hedgewar and his friends supported him financially, and made all the arrangements for his daughter's wedding. At his daughter's wedding, Hedgewar personally supervised all the arrangements.

Hussain was a devout follower of Lokmanya Tilak, and had taken the vow of swadeshi. He also ran a swadeshi provision store called 'Kuber Vastu Bhandar'.

When Hussain was severely ill, Hedgewar personally nursed him and was constantly by his bedside for two months.

How RSS got its Name

Though the RSS was founded on the day of 'Vijayadashami' in 1925 but the name of the organisation was decided much later.

On 17 April 1926, Hedgewar called for a meeting attended by 26 swayamsevaks. A detailed discussion followed to decide the name of the organisation.

Three names were finalised after several rounds of elimination—RSS, Jaripataka Mandal and Bhedratoddharak Mandal.

There were more deliberations on these three names and finally the name, 'RSS', was chosen.

❑

24

Golwalkar: The Man who Transformed RSS to a Pan-India Organisation

With more than 60,000 daily shakhas, around 4000 full-time pracharaks and three dozen organisations run by its volunteers working in every sphere of society if Rashtriya Swayam Sevak Sengh (RSS) has emerged as the largest voluntary movement across the world, MS Golwalkar played one of the most crucial roles in it.

The RSS attained a truly pan-Indian character by expanding rapidly from 1940 to 1973 under his leadership even as the organisation went through some of the most tumultuous events happening in the country such as partition, ban on the RSS, India's debacle in 1962 war, India-Pakistan wars in 1965 and 1971. Golwalkar ensured that not only RSS got over the ban imposed on it in 1948 but he stewarded the organisation to a greater ideological clarity and stronger organisational structure.

Born on 19 February 1906 at Ramtek in

Maharashtra, MS Golwalkar, was the second Sarsanghchalak of RSS. He took over this responsibility in 1940 and worked in the same capacity till he took the last breath in 1973.

MS Golwalkar is commonly known as 'Guruji'. He got this name when he was working in Banaras Hindu University for a couple of years. The students used to call him 'Guruji' fondly and the name stuck.

According to the information available with the RSS archives, Guruji is known to have travelled across the whole country more than 65 times to set up RSS-inspired organisations in every field and sector ranging from tribal welfare to student politics.

In 1930 while teaching at Banaras Hindu University where he had studied, he came in contact with the RSS for the first time through Bhaiyaji Dani, who had arrived in Kashi in 1928 for further studies and had started a Shakha there.

Interestingly, around a decade later, when Guruji became Sarsanghachalak, Dani worked as Sarkaryavaha (General Secretary) for some years. It was Guruji who used to take swayamsevaks to meet Pandit Madan Mohan Malaviya at the BHU campus.

In 1934 he was appointed Karyawaha (Secretary in-charge) of the Sangh's main Shakha which was being held at Tulsibagh at that time. He was also sent to Mumbai in 1934 by Dr Hedgewar to spread the organisation's work there. In 1935, he was appointed as the Sarvadhikari (the overall chief) of the RSS training camp held at Akola.

At a function, to celebrate the festival of Raksha Bandhan in 1939, Dr KB Hedgewar, the founder of RSS, announced Guruji's appointment as the Sarkaryavaha (General Secretary).

Guruji held the post of Sarkaryavaha for only ten months. During this time, the RSS outreach expanded to Madhya Pradesh, Maharashtra and even distant places like Punjab, Delhi, Karachi, Patna, Calcutta, Lucknow etc. A few days after the death of Dr Hedgewar, a meeting of five Sanghchalaks took place in Akola, attended among others by Appaji Joshi, Babasaheb Ghatate and Maharashtra Sanghachalak Kashinathrao Limaye. The meeting reviewed the situation and everyone agreed that Guruji is the right successor.

In June 1940, the Sangh began its journey under the extraordinary ideological and organisational stewardship of Guruji. Although, the Sangh had spread out to some provinces outside Maharashtra, several parts of the country still remained untouched.

Till now, the RSS volunteers started shakhas wherever they went as students. There were only a handful of pracharaks. Guruji started the system of having full-time workers (pracharaks) sent exclusively to expand the organisation's work. The result was a phenomenal growth in the organisation's network across the country.

His appeal to young swayamsevaks in 1941 and 1942 was, "We need Pracharaks...we need pracharaks. This is the demand arising from all directions. We must fulfil this demand."

The impact of Guruji's clarion call was phenomenal. Forty-eight pracharaks came just from Lahore in 1942. Of these, 10 had passed M.A., two were doctors, 14 shastris and others were B.A. graduates and those above matric. Similarly, 52 pracharaks came from Amritsar city and there were four doctors amongst them.

A CID report dated 30 December 1943 said, "RSS is moving ahead rapidly towards building a highly significant all-India organisation....a new dimension to their growth is their efforts to gain entry in the villages. MS Golwalkar laid a lot of stress on this aspect in the winter camp of Wardha—that the Sangh should expand into villages...We can see the recent well spread-out tour of the present chief of the Sangh, MS Golwalkar as an example of such efforts. In the last month of April, he was in Ahmedabad; in May, he was at Amravati and Pune. In June, he was at Nasik and Benaras. He toured Chanda in August, Pune in September, Madras and Central Provinces in October and Rawalpindi in November..."

In run-up to the partition of India, the RSS realised the need to prepare the Hindus to face the inevitable that had been imposed on them by the Congress leadership. Guruji, Babasaheb Apte and Balasaheb Deoras extensively toured the country. Guruji went to Sialkot and Montgomery after touring Multan in 1946-47. He entered Sindh from Punjab. The province of Sindh had around 80 Shakhas at that time. There were 52 pracharaks that included Lal Krishna Advani. During partition, RSS saved millions of Hindus from areas where they were stuck in Pakistan. The English Tribune wrote, "If Punjab is the sword arm of India, RSS is the sword arm of Punjab."

Ban on RSS

On 30 January 1948, Mahatma Gandhi was assassinated in New Delhi. Guruji was in Chennai. On the same day, he passed instructions from Chennai to all the Shakhas, "To express our grief due to the sad demise of respected Mahatmaji, Shakhas will observe a condolence period for 13 days and all daily programmes will be put on hold." He left for Nagpur on 31 January by air.

Guruji was arrested on 2 February and the RSS was banned on 4 February through a central government notification.

Nearly 20,000 swayamsevaks were arrested across the country. On 6 August Guruji was released from the jail but with several conditions including restricting his movements within the municipal limit of Nagpur.

Guruji was again arrested at midnight of 12 November 1948, at Barakhamba Road, Delhi under the Bengal State Criminal Procedure Act of 1818. On his call, a satyagraha was carried out for 45 days from 9 December 1948 to 22 January 1949 by the RSS volunteers. More than 77,000 swayamsevaks courted arrest and were sent to prison. Later, Guruji was shifted to Baitul prison. The ban on the RSS was lifted on midnight of 11 July 1949. Guruji was released on 13 July 1949 from Baitul prison.

Meanwhile the RSS took up a major relief and rehabilitation effort in West Bengal to address the issue of Hindu refugees from East Pakistan. At the behest of Guruji, 'Vastuhara Sahaayata Samiti' (Displaced People's Relief Committee) was constituted under the chairmanship of Barrister Ranadev Chaudhary on 8 February 1950. Many pracharaks were deputed from the nearby states to help these refugees. Eknath Ranade was entrusted to drive this initiative. Guruji himself visited Kolkata to assess the situation.

The year 1952 saw Guruji inspiring swayamsevaks to move into the field of education by setting up a model of Swadeshi education. There were detailed discussions between Guruji and Professor Rajendra Singh (who later became fourth Sarsanghchalak), Nanaji Deshmukh, Pandit Deendayal Upadhyaya, Bhaurao Deoras on this issue.

As a result, the first Saraswati Shishu Mandir came into existence under the leadership of Nanaji Deshmukh at Gorakhpur. Guruji laid the foundation stone of the building. Today this movement has more than 20,000 schools in the country educating more than 3.5 million students.

In 1952, the RSS also launched the Cow Protection movement. The Akhil Bharatiya Pratinidhi Sabha (the highest decision-making body of the RSS) passed a resolution in Nagpur in September, 1952 about banning cow slaughter across the country.

The RSS volunteers collected signatures from 94,459 villages and towns. Total count of signatures was one crore seventy-nine lakh eighty-nine thousand three hundred thirty-two (1,79,89,332). On 8 December 1952, Guruji met the President of India to hand over these signatures seeking a ban on cow slaughter.

One of the key impacts of the Cow protection campaign was that it galvanised the RSS at an organisational level and increased its organisational reach significantly.

The RSS was now getting increasingly involved in the relief and rehabilitation efforts wherever a disaster or calamity struck in the country. This resulted in setting up of the 'Seva Vibhag' (a wing for Social Services).

In 1952, India witnessed its first General Elections. Dr Syama Prasad Mookerjee had resigned from Nehru's cabinet in protest against his policies. The former was thinking of setting up a new political party. He met Guruji, Balasaheb Deoras and Bhaurao Deoras in early 1951 at the home of Nagpur Sanghchalak Babasaheb Ghatate. It was decided to launch Bharatiya Jana Sangh after the discussions. The RSS loaned out some of its pracharaks to help the cause of setting up a nationalist party while making it clear that the RSS would not be involved directly in any political activity. So pracharaks like Deendayal Upadhyaya, Atal Bihari Vajpayee and Nanaji Deshmukh got associated with the Bharatiya Jana Sangh with Dr Mookerjee at the helm of affairs.

One of the stalwarts and leading ideologues of the RSS, Dattopant Thengadi founded the Bharatiya

Mazdoor Sangh (BMS) on 23 July 1955. Interestingly, Thengadi learnt the ropes of labour movement in Congress-backed INTUC. Today, BMS is the largest labour organisation/trade union in the country.

In the year 1960, Guruji warned the government of the day about a possible foreign aggression and in 1962, China attacked India. The RSS came out in full force to defend the nation and help the government to fight this aggression.

The then Prime Minister Nehru had to recognise the value of RSS' efforts despite being a staunch opponent of the organisation. He invited an RSS contingent to participate in the Republic Day Parade in Delhi in 1963. Around 3,000 RSS swayamsevaks participated in that march.

In 1965, when Pakistan attacked India, the then PM Lal Bahadur Shastri, invited Guruji for an all-party consultative committee meeting in Delhi even though the RSS was a non-political entity. The RSS extended complete support to the government. Disagreeing with the way, the ceasefire had been declared suddenly, Guruji was also of the opinion that it was not desirable for Shastri to go to Tashkent for negotiations. Shastri died a mysterious death in Tashkent.

Meanwhile, from late 1940s onwards RSS volunteers had moved in various fields setting up a number of organisations such as Akhil Bharatiya Vidyarthi Parishad (ABVP) and Vanvasi Kalyan Ashram.

A decision to set up Vishva Hindu Parishad (VHP)

was taken in 1964. The VHP organised first world Hindu Conference at Prayag in 1966 during Kumbha Mela. Prior to this convention, a senior RSS pracharak Dadasaheb Apte had gone on a world tour to garner support for setting up this organisation at the behest of Guruji. Guruji addressed the first convention of VHP. It was VHP which spearheaded the Ram Temple movement from 1980s onwards.

In May, 1970, Guruji was diagnosed with cancer. On 1 July 1970 he underwent a three-hour surgery. While being at hospital, he started visiting a nearby RSS Shakha. He also attended the annual meeting of the RSS' Central Executive Committee at Mumbai from 10–12 July. On 26 July he left the hospital and on 3 August he left for Nagpur by train.

The RSS' Central Executive met at Nagpur from 8–10 July 1971 and passed a resolution on the situation in Bangladesh, calling upon the Government to keep its solemn promise given to the Hindus of Pakistan at the time of partition, assuring them of safety and security.

On 3 December 1971 Pakistan attacked India. At that time, a training camp for young swayamsevaks was in progress in Nagpur. Guruji immediately issued a statement regarding the aggression and the corresponding responsibility of the citizens. Lakhs of copies of his statement were distributed from door to door by the swayamsevaks.

In his statement, issued on 4 December1971 Guruji appealed to the countrymen, "The unity inspired by genuine love for the motherland alone can lead us to victory. Pakistan is at war with us. Our government and the army are quite capable of meeting the challenge, but it is essential to keep the morale of the people high and maintain highest levels of production in fields and factories. Besides, our Jawans on the front must feel that the entire nation is behind them. Civil defence, blood donations, nursing of wounded personnel etc., are some of the essential services to be organised forthwith."

After India's victory, he sent a letter to the then Prime Minister Indira Gandhi on 22 December saying, "In the creation of the strength of national unity infused with national pride, the RSS is and will always be with you. I have confidence that as the representative of the country you will take all these factors into consideration while determining our domestic and foreign policies. May the prestige of Bharat grow like this under your leadership."

After the war, Guruji expressed his deep reservations about the Shimla Accord. As his health continued to deteriorate, on 2 April 1973, he wrote three letters in his own hand and handed them over to the office secretary, Pandurang Kshirasagar.

On 5 June 1973, he passed away. The three letters Guruji had given to Kshirasagar were opened in the presence of senior functionaries of the RSS. In one of the letters, he had entrusted the Sarsanghachalak's responsibility to Balasaheb Deoras. In another letter he had directed that there should be no memorial to him. In the third letter, he had quoted a prayer by the saint Tukaram.

"Oh saints and holy men, convey this my final prayer to God. Oh God! do not forget me. What more can I say? You, my Lord, know everything. I bow to you...

Take me into the shelter of your Grace."

❑

25

RSS and Mahatma Gandhi's Assassination: Myths vs Facts

Detractors of the Rashtriya Swayamsevak Sangh have often accused it of Mahatma Gandhi's assassination. The facts, however, tell a different story.

What is that story?

RSS' second Sarsanghchalak MS Golwalkar was attending an RSS meeting in Chennai when Gandhi was assassinated. Around half an hour after the assassination of Mahatma Gandhi on 30 January 1948, an FIR was lodged at the Tughlak Road police station.

The FIR contains a statement from Nand Lal Mehta, a resident of Connaught Place in Delhi. Mehta was reportedly standing next to Gandhi when he was shot.

Here is what Mehta had to say: "Today, I was present at Birla House. Around 10 minutes past five in the evening, Mahatma Gandhi left his room in Birla House for the prayer ground. Sister Abha Gandhi and Sister Sanno Gandhi were accompanying him. Mahatma was walking with his hands on the shoulders of the two sisters. Two more girls were there in the group. I along with Lala Brij Kishan, a silver merchant, resident of No. 1, Narendra Place, Parliament Street and Sardar Gurbachan Singh, resident of Timar Pur, Delhi were also there. Apart from us, women from the Birla household and two–three members of the staff were also present. Having crossed the garden, Mahatma climbed the concrete steps towards the prayer place. People were standing on both the sides and approximately three feet of vacant space was left for the Mahatma to pass through. As per the custom, the Mahatma greeted the people with folded hands. He had barely covered six or seven steps when a person whose name I learnt later as Narayan Vinayak Godse, resident of Poona, stepped closer and fired three shots from a pistol at the Mahatma from barely 2-3 feet distance which hit the Mahatma in his stomach and chest and blood started flowing. Mahatma ji fell backwards, uttering 'Ram–Ram'. The assailant was apprehended on the spot with the weapon. The Mahatma was carried away in an unconscious state towards the residential unit of the Birla House where he passed away instantly and the police took away the assailant..."

Even as this FIR was being lodged, RSS chief MS Golwalkar was attending an RSS meeting in Chennai (then known as Madras). A number of prominent citizens were present in the meeting. According to an eyewitness, just when the RSS chief was about to take the first sip of the tea offered to him, someone broke the news about Gandhi's death.

As soon as he heard the news, he put down his cup and said in an anguished voice, "What a misfortune for the country!"

He immediately sent telegrams of condolences to the then Prime Minister Jawaharlal Nehru, Union home minister Sardar Vallabhbhai Patel and Devdas Gandhi, the fourth and youngest son of Mahatma Gandhi.

The RSS chief cancelled his countrywide tour and flew back to the RSS headquarters in Nagpur.

In an unprecedented move, all RSS shakhas were asked to be closed for 13 days to mourn Gandhi's demise.

Since the organisation's inception in1925, shakhas were held 365 days a year without any break. That is the core principle of the RSS. However, the organisation made an exception for Gandhi—this shows the respect Gandhi commanded in the RSS.

Golwalkar, after returning to Nagpur, wrote to Nehru, "The attack on such a deft helmsman, who held so many diverse natures in a single string bringing them to the right path, is indeed a treacherous act not merely to an individual but to the whole country. No doubt you, that is, the government authorities of the day, will deal suitably with that traitorous individual. But now is a testing time for all of us. The responsibility of safely steering the ship of our nation ahead in the present troubled times with an unruffled sense of judgement, sweetness of speech and single-minded devotion to the nation's interest is upon all of us."

The RSS chief also wrote to the deputy PM Sardar Patel. He said, "Let us shoulder the responsibility that has fallen upon us by the untimely passing away of that great unifier, keeping alive the sacred memories of that soul who had tied diverse natures in a single bond and was leading them all on a single path. And let us, with the right feelings, restrained tone and fraternal love, conserve our strength and cement the national life with everlasting oneness."

However, in a knee-jerk reaction, the government banned the RSS on 4 February 1948, and arrested Golwalkar.

Ironically, the arrest was made under the notorious Bengal State Prisoners Act. Nehru had condemned this act before independence as a 'black law'.

The RSS chief was released six months later but was arrested again after some time. A satyagraha by the RSS swayamsevaks followed. More than 77,000 RSS volunteers courted arrest. The government of the day could not find any evidence against the RSS.

In fact, a month after Gandhi's assassination, Sardar Patel reportedly wrote to Nehru, "I have kept myself almost in daily touch with the progress of the investigations regarding Bapu's assassination case. All main accused have given long and detailed statements of their activities. It also clearly emerges from the statements that the RSS was not involved in it at all."

In another letter to the RSS chief, Sardar Patel said, "Only the people near me know as to how happy I was when the ban on Sangh was lifted. I wish you all the best."

The ban on the RSS was lifted on 12 July 1949.

However, RSS baiters continued to spread the canard about the organisation's role in Gandhi's assassination.

In 1966, the Congress government headed by Prime Minister Indira Gandhi again set up a new judicial commission to thoroughly probe the assassination. Justice JL Kapur, a retired judge of the Supreme Court, headed it. The commission examined 101 witnesses and 407 documents. The panel's report was published in 1969. Its key findings were:

(a) They (the accused) have not been proved to have been members of the RSS, nor has that organisation been shown to have had a hand in the murder. (Volume I, page 186)

(b) There is no evidence that the RSS as such was indulging in violent activities against Mahatma Gandhi or the top Congress leaders. (Volume I, page 66)

One of the most important witnesses who deposed before the Kapur Commission was an Indian Civil Services officer called RN Banerjee. His deposition was crucial as he was the home secretary to the government of India at the time of the assassination.

Banerjee told the Kapur Commission that even if the RSS had been banned earlier, it would not have affected the conspirators or the course of events, "because they have not been proved to have been members of the RSS, nor has that organisation been shown to have a hand in the murder."

❑

26

Lessons that can be Learnt from Tagore on Hindu Dharma

A look at some of the thoughts expressed by Nobel Laureate and one of the most towering national icons of India, Rabindranath Tagore in one of his relatively less talked about articles titled 'Swadeshi Samaj' reveals how he looked at resolving conflicts through Hindu Dharma. He had expressed these thoughts in lectures delivered twice in the early years of 20th century in Bengal, which was later on published as a long article.

Tagore talked about the importance of shunning violence as a tool to dominate the rivals and the resilience of India's ancient heritage, Hindu dharma and the importance of 'Hindu viewpoint' as the only way out to resolve conflict in the Indian society.

According to 'Introduction' to the English translation of this article done by Anasuya Guha and published by Dey's Publishing in the form of book titled 'Swadeshi Samaj' by Rabindranath Tagore' (2013), "The article was first read out on the 7th of

Shravan, Friday, Bengali 1311 at the special meeting of Chaitanya Library at Minerva Theatre. Later, on 16th Shravan Bengali 1311 an enlarged edition of this was again read at Curzon Theatre."

Tagore said in the first lecture, "Each fresh conflict will enable us to expand ourselves. The Hindu, the Buddhist, the Muslim and the Christian will not fight each other and die in India. Here they will find a meeting point."

Emphasising the importance of a 'Hindu viewpoint', he further added, "That meeting point will not be non-Hindu but very specifically Hindu. However foreign may be her body parts, her life and spirit will be India's."

Referring to the uselessness of attempts to dominate through force and violence from which the perpetrators of ongoing violence in West Bengal can learn a bit or two, Tagore underlined, "To feel unity in diversity, to establish unity amidst variety—this the underlying religion of India. India does not regard difference as hostility, she does not regard the other as enemy. That is why without sacrifice or destruction she wants to accommodate everybody within the great system. That is why she accepts all ways and sees the greatness of each in his own sphere."

Further, talking about the use of power to dominate others, he shares a lesson from which many can learn today. "India has never fought over kingdom, squabbled over trade. Tibet, China or Japan who are willing to close all doors and windows in fear of great Europe, that same Tibet, China and Japan have beckoned India inside in their home in an unworried fashion as guru or religious leader. India has not traumatised the whole world's flesh and blood with her own army and goods, but has squired the esteem of mankind by establishing peace, consolation and religious systems everywhere. Thus, the glory she has acquired has been done through penance and it is greater than the glory of the sovereignty over other kingdoms."

"If we keep in mind this divine dispensation for India, then we shall have a fixed target, our diffidence will be removed and we shall know about that deathless force in India. We have to remember that we shall not only receive the European knowledge as pupils, the Indian Saraswati will make all factions and conflicts bloom like a hundred petalled lotus and will remove its fragmentation. The main duty of the Indian genius is to bring about unity. India is not one to keep others at a distance or to forsake others. India will one day indicate to this contentious divided world how to accept all and receive all and how to establish each within one great nation."

Talking about the importance of reviving the ancient heritage as a way forward for the Indian society, Tagore said, "If you are able to revive that heart of our ancestors to lead this static society of ours, only then shall we be great. If our entire society becomes alive and active rejuvenated by the noble moments and greatness of the ancient times, if it makes self strong and mobile with the life force of centuries crossing through its organs then foreign rule and all other kinds of misery will become trifling matters."

Giving a befitting reply to the critics of Hindu dharma, Tagore said, "Today many may ask: Where is the unity in this Hindu society, in this Hindu religion prone to internal feud and schisms? It is difficult to supply a clear answer. It is equally difficult to find the epicentre of a great periphery. But it definitely has one. It is not difficult to comprehend the spherical quality of a sphere. But those who perceive the spherical earth in small segments, would regard it as a flat. Similarly, the Hindu society has harmonized many mutually contradictory elements of variety so that the source of unity has become abtruse and concealed. It is difficult to lay one's finger on this Unity but it is easy to feel this Unity existing strongly within all the apparently perceived contradictions."

❑

27

Maharaja Hari Singh: The True Patriot

Six decades after the death of Maharaja Hari Singh of Jammu and Kashmir, the man who signed treaty of accession with India, there are certain aspects of his public life which have not been discussed much, hence promoting certain stereotypes by him. With no love lost between him and the Abdullahs of National Conference, the Maharaja, contrary to the reality, was not projected as a patriot. The fact is that he always wanted his state to accede to India and shunned several Pakistani efforts to compel him to be part of Pakistan.

Justice Mehr Chand Mahajan, who took over as Prime Minister of Jammu and Kashmir on 15 October 1947 on request of then Home Minister Sardar Vallabhbhai Patel has recalled in his autobiography 'Looking Back"' the patriotism and pro-India feelings of the Maharaja. Incidentally, Mahajan was given a leave of eight months from Punjab High Court to be appointed as the PM of Jammu and Kashmir. He later became the Chief Justice of India also.

Mahajan writes, "Prior to my taking over as Prime Minister, Mr (Mohammad Ali) Jinnah had on three occasions made attempts to come to Srinagar and stay there, ostensibly for reasons of health. He had sent his military secretary, a Britisher, twice with a personal letter to the Maharaja with the request that as advised by his physicians he should be allowed to visit the valley. He was willing to come as a private citizen and to make his own arrangement for his stay."

"The Maharaja suspected that the object of his visit to Srinagar was to coerce him so as to secure Kashmir's accession to Pakistan, to take possession of the state and to celebrate the festival of Eid there as the Governor General of Pakistan, including Kashmir. The Maharaja sent a polite refusal to all his requests emphasising the fact, that he being the Governor General of Pakistan could only visit the state if due arrangements could be made for his stay there by the State government according to his status as head of a neighbouring state, and if proper security arrangements were possible. This, the Maharaja said, he was not able to do in the circumstances that had arisen," added Justice (retd.) Mahajan.

According to him, "If the Maharaja had not turned down the request, Mr Jinnah would have somehow created a situation in Kashmir leading to its accession to Pakistan and its final annexation. Mr Jinnah had openly proclaimed that legally speaking, the question of accession depended entirely on the choice of the ruler and the people of state had no right to question his choice. The Maharaja was being constantly told that he was an independent sovereign, that he needed to consult nobody in the matter of accession of the State. After accession to Pakistan, he could continue to be an absolute ruler of the state. "

Justice Mahajan also made an interesting observation about Sheikh Abdullah, who was considered to be close to the then Prime Minister Jawaharlal Nehru and a major reason for strained relationship between Nehru and Maharaja Hari Singh. "...my first good look at Sheikh Abdullah and my impression was that he was out to gain power at any cost. To acquire it he would try to influence his friend, the Prime Minister of India..."

And that is what happened too. Nehru's insistence on handing over the reins of Jammu-Kashmir administration to Sheikh Abdullah was one of the key reasons for delay in the signing of Instrument of Accession by Maharaja Hari Singh.

Golwalkar's Role

In fact, it is also said that the second Sarsanghchalak of Rashtriya Swayamsevak Sangh (RSS), Madhav Sadashiv Golwalkar, popularly known as 'Guruji' played an important role in convincing Maharaja to sign the instrument of accession.

Guruji reached Srinagar by air from Delhi on 17 October 1947. The meeting between him and Maharaja Hari Singh took place on the morning of 18 October where Guruji convinced Maharaja to integrate his state with India without any further delay. Former bureaucrat and close aide of Sonia Gandhi during United Progressive Alliance's (UPA) regime, Arun Bhatnagar has also mentioned this incident in his book 'India: Shedding the Past, Embracing the Future, 1906-2017'. Bhatnagar, a 1966 batch IAS officer has written that Guruji went to meet Maharaja Hari Singh after he was urged by Sardar Patel to take up this matter. Madhavrao Mule, who was the RSS' Prant Pracharak (Full-time worker and in-charge of a province) of Jammu and Kashmir and Punjab at that time has also explained this incident in detail in his book 'Shri Guruji Samagra Darshan'.

❑

28

Praja Parishad Party: The Unsung Heroes of Jammu & Kashmir

Few would know, it was a non-descript political outfit in Jammu and Kashmir, the Praja Parishad Party, that prepared the ground for the kashmir policy of Narondra Modi government.

The ground work for amendment of Article 370 and removal of Section 35A changing the complete political and constitutional landscape of the state (which is now a Union Territory) can be traced back to 14 November, 1952 when the first 'satyagraha' in Jammu and Kashmir was launched by the unsung heroes of a political outfit 'Praja Parishad Party' which went down quietly into annals of the history. In fact, before even Bharatiya Jana Sangh (BJS), which later transformed into BJP, had made abrogation of Article 370 its key agenda, it was the Praja Parishad Party who fought for 11 long years with this demand paving the way for what happened on 5 August, 2019 when Article 370 was amended, Section 35 A was scrapped and Jammu and Kashmir was reorganised into two Union Territories–Jammu & Kashmir and Ladakh.

Praja Parsihad was founded on 17 November, 1947 in Jammu with Hari Vazir as its first president and Hansraj Pangotra as the general secretary. But the real force behind formation of this party and its subsequent agitational politics were two members of the RSS— Balraj Madhok and Prem Nath Dogra.

The Party launched its first formal 'Satyagraha' demanding complete integration of Jammu and Kashmir with India on 14 November, 1952. The core demand of the movement was to have no special constitutional provisions and separate flag for Jammu and Kashmir. Popularly, the slogan in Hindi to reflect these demands which became the battle cry for Praja Parishad's agitation was 'Ek desh mein do Vidhan, do pradhan, do nishan nahin chaleinge, nahin chaleinge' (It is not acceptable to have two constitutions, two heads of state and twoflogs in one covntry.)

The first salvo of this movement was launched by Praja Parishad on 17 November, when Karan Singh, son of Maharaja Hari Singh took the oath of Sadre-Riyasat at Polo Ground in Srinagar. A separate flag for the state was to be unfurled at the state government secretariat in Jammu but due to Praja Parishad's protests, this could not be done. That was the first victory for this outfit which had locked the horns with state government led by Sheikh Abdullah as well as the Nehru government at the Centre, on this issue.

On 26 November 1952, Prem Nath Dogra, 68, courted the first arrest under this movement in Jammu after addressing a public meeting. This arrest was immediately followed by lathi charge on the crowd and arrest of seven more persons including Om Prakash Maingi, the president of Jammu unit. The agitation soon spread to Kathua, Samba, Udhampur and other parts of the state.

On 2 December1952, the first firing incident happened where the state police fired on agitationists in Udhampur, around 300 persons were injured but no casualty was reported. More than 50 persons were arrested.

Exactly a month after the beginning of this agitation, the first casualty happened. Mela Ram, one of the satyagrahis, was shot dead by police as he was trying to hoist India's national flag at headquarters of Chhamb tehsil. More than 30,000 people participated in his funeral indicating the widespread influence of the movement. Two weeks after this incident, three more styagrahis succumbed to police firing as they tried to unfurl the tricolour at Sundarbani tehsil in Poonch district.

The Praja Parishad workers decided to take the agitation nationwide. On 18 and 19 December they reached and distributed pamphlets at the Congress Party's annual convention in Hyderabad in the presence of Prime Minister Jawaharlal Nehru and the National Conference leader Sheikh Abdullah. The leaders of Praja Parishad also got in touch with newly formed BJS led by Dr Syama Prasad Mookerjee.

Meanwhile, Karan Singh wrote to Nehru on 4 January1953, "It has been one and a half month since this movement had started but I feel sad that no positive steps have been taken so far by the government."

On 11 January 1953, two days before the festival of Lohri, the police fired upon a march in which more than 5,000 people were participating. They wanted to submit a memorandum to the then deputy prime minister of Jammu and Kashmir Bakshi Ghulam Mohammad who was visiting Hiranagar. More than 200 rounds were fired, two persons were killed and more than 70 were injured.

On 16 January, 1953, Praja Parishad formally launched the civil disobedience movement. On 30 January, a crowd of 3,000 protesters gathered at Jodian village. The police fired upon them in which six persons were killed, around 125 people were injured and many went missing.

On 1 March 1953, three protesters were killed in police firing at Ramban court complex as they tried to mount the Tricolour, India's national flag there.

Meanwhile the BJS, Hindu Mahasabha and Akali dal launched a nationwide agitation to support Praja Parishad on 5 March1953. The BJS President, Syama Prasad Mookerjee left for Jammu and Kashmir on a train from New Delhi on 8 May 1953 to support the agitation there. He was arrested while trying to enter Jammu and Kashmir on 11 May. He was detained in Srinagar for more than a month where he died under mysterious circumstances on 23 June 1953.

Prime Minister Nehru appealed to Praja Parishad

to call off this agitation in the wake of this tragedy. The latter decided to call of the civil disobedience movement on 7 July 1953. But it continued with the movement to have a common Constitution and flag till it got merged with BJS on 30 December 1963. Later BJS and then from 1980 onwards the BJP, the new avatar of BJS, carried forward these demands. On 5 August 2019, these demands were finally fulfilled.

(The information above has been sourced from 'Jammu-Kashmir Ki Ankahi Kahani' by Dr Kuldeep Chandra Agnihotri and 'Pledge for an Integrated India: Dr Mookerjee in throes of Jammu and Kashmir' ed. by Devesh Khandelwal).

❑

29

Moplah Riots: An 'Anti-Hindu Genocide'

In the run up to the centenary year of the infamous Moplah rebellion (1921-22), an almost forgotten chapter of Indian history, a major ideological debate started brewing following the announcement in June, 2020 of a Malayalam movie on the issue.

'Variyamkunnan' was set to be a biopic on Variyamkunnath Kunjahammed Haji, one of the key controversial figures in the rebellion. The movie, expected to be released in the centenary year of Moplah rebellion in 2021, was announced to be directed by Aashiq Abu, with actor Prithviraj in the titular role.

It promised to portray a positive image of Haji but not everyone was buying it.

Criticising the attempt "to glorify Haji" and by extension the Moplah rebellion, J. Nandakumar, an RSS pracharak and national convenor of the Prajna Pravah, an organisation that works among intellectuals, said the rebellion was nothing but Hindu genocide.

"The protagonist of this Islamist project, Kunjahammed Haji, belonged to a rabidly iconoclastic family. His father was earlier deported to Mecca for engineering a slew of communal riots," Nandakumar said.

"He spearheaded the Hindu genocide of 1921, which led to the massacre of thousands of Hindus, forcible conversions, rape of Hindu women and children and destruction of Hindu properties and places of worship.

"Reportedly, in the biopic, Kunjahammed is projected as a paragon of communal harmony and Hindus as villains who sided with the British. And that his 'valiant efforts' led to the flight of the British from that part of the country and he established an independent Malayala Nadu (land of Malayalis) for a few months," he added.

"In reality, what he established was Al-Daula (Islamic State) where he imposed jizya (religious tax) on the Hindus of his territory."

The violence in the region began at Tirurangadi in Kerala's South Malabar on 20 August, 1921, and lasted for over four months, resulting in the imposition of martial law in six out of ten taluks in the then Malabar district. More than a lakh Hindus were displaced.

"It was the Marxist historians who first appropriated the communal pogrom as a peasant uprising to suit their ideological narratives and requirements and win over a large organised vote-bank for the Left parties," Nandakumar said.

This peasant uprising theory has been constantly challenged and the debate is likely to get back on the national agenda.

The genocids that united Savarkar, Ambedkar & Annie Besant

Vinayak Damodar Savarkar was one of the first ones to describe the Moplah rebellion as an anti-Hindu genocide through his semi-fictional novel 'Moplah', which became hugely popular when it was published in 1924.

According to another book, 'The Moplah Rebellion', Haji was an outlaw who played a key role in the rebellion. The book, published in 1923, and put together by the then deputy collector of the area, C. Gopalan Nair, is considered to be one of the most authentic accounts of the event.

"Murders, dacoities, forced conversions and outrages on Hindu women became order of the day," recorded Nair in his book.

Even Dr BR Ambedkar has provided a detailed account on the rebellion in 'Pakistan or The Partition of India' (Dr Babasaheb Ambedkar, Writings and Speeches, Volume 8, P.163), and it is not a glowing one.

"Beginning with the year 1920 there occurred in that year in Malabar what is known as the Mopla Rebellion. It was the result of the agitation carried out by two Muslim organisations, the Khuddam-i-Kaba (servants of the Mecca Shrine) and the Central Khilafat Committee," Ambedkar wrote.

"Agitators actually preached the doctrine that India under the British Government was Dar-ul-Harab and that the Muslims must fight against it and if they could not, they must carry out the alternative principle of Hijrat. The Moplas were suddenly carried off their feet by this agitation. The outbreak was essentially a rebellion against the British Government. The aim was to establish the kingdom of Islam by overthrowing the British Government."

"As a rebellion against the British Government it was quite understandable. But what baffled most was the treatment accorded by the Moplas to the Hindus of Malabar," he wrote.

"The Hindus were visited by a dire fate at the hands of the Moplas. Massacres, forcible conversions, desecration of temples, foul outrages upon women, such as ripping open pregnant women, pillage, arson and destruction—in short, all the accompaniments of brutal and unrestrained barbarism, were perpetrated freely by the Moplas upon the Hindus until such time as troops could be hurried to the task of restoring order through a difficult and extensive tract of the country."

"This was not a Hindu-Moslem riot. This was just a Bartholomew. The number of Hindus who were killed, wounded or converted, is not known. But the number must have been enormous," wrote Ambedkar.

It took more than four months for the British to

control the rebellion. The official records show 2,266 killed, 1,615 wounded, 5,688 captured, while 38,256 surrendered during military engagements.

Theosophist and one of the most respected figures in India's struggle for freedom during the 20th century, Annie Besant, who had presided over the first 'Reform Conference' in Malabar in the spring of 1921, also wrote in detail about the event.

"The fourfold programme was begun formally on August 1, 1920; Swaraj was to be attained in a year, and on August 1, 1921, the first step was taken in the Malabar Rebellion; the Musalmans (Moplas) of that district after three weeks of preparing weapons, rose over a definite area in revolt, believing, as they had been told, that British Rule had ceased, and they were free," she wrote in 'The Future of Indian Politics' (Theosophical Publishing House,1922, p. 252).

"They established the Khilafat Raj, crowned a King, murdered and plundered abundantly, and killed or drove away all Hindus who would not apostatise. Somewhere about a lakh people were driven from their homes with nothing but the clothes they had on, stripped of everything," she added.

❑

30

Savarkar and Bhagat Singh: The Close Connect

Two of the most talked about revolutionaries in India's struggle for freedom—Bhagat Singh and Vinayak Damodar Savarkar (popularly known as Veer Savarkar) —not only respected each other but they had a strong emotional bond that connected them. They revered each other, and Savarkar was an inspiration for Bhagat Singh.

Historical records show that Bhagat Singh considered Savarkar to be a role model as a revolutionary and Savarkar was in deep grief when Bhagat Singh was hanged along with Rajguru and Sukhdev on 23 March 1931 by the British Government.

'Matwala', a patriotic Hindi weekly, which used to be published from Calcutta, carried an article titled 'Vishwa Prem' written by Bhagat Singh. The article was in its two issues on 15 and 22 November, 1926. Praising Savarkar and countering his critics, Bhagat Singh wrote, "The one who loves this world is that braveheart, whom we don't hesitate to call as a fierce insurgent and a fanatic anarchist—this is the Veer (brave) Savarkar." This article was written under the pseudonym of Balwant Singh and can be found in 'Bhagat Singh aur unke sathiyon ke sampoorna uplabhda dastawej' (Complete available documents of Bhagat Singh and his fellow revolutionaries, 2019, Rahul Foundation, Page 93).

When Bhagat Singh wrote this article, Savarkar was under house arrest at Ratnagiri in Maharashtra. He was prohibited from participating in any political activity after release from Cellular Jail in the Andamans, infamously called 'Kala Paani' in those days. Many critics of Savarkar have questioned his release on the condition that he would not participate in the political activities further. Bhagat Singh's thoughts during that era clearly shows that the revolutionaries clearly understood that it was Savarkar's tactical decision to accept this pre-condition of the British Government so that he could come out of the prison to continue to participate in India's freedom struggle instead of languishing in a far away prison.

In August 1928, Bhagat Singh published an article in 'Keerti', another well-known publication of revolutionaries. This article was penned as a part of a series of articles written by Bhagat Singh on the lives of various Indian revolutionaries so that readers could understand how the freedom struggle against the British shaped and evolved especially in Punjab. This series of articles was published from March 1928 to October 1928. It was titled 'Azadi Ki Shahadtein' (Sacrifices on the altar of freedom).

While writing about Madan Lal Dhingra, who shot dead Curzon Wylie in England, Bhagat Singh wrote in detail how Savarkar had set up 'India House' which became the hub of Indian revolutionaries and then how Savarkar inspired Dhingra to go ahead on his mission fearlessly. Explaining the emotional moments when Dhingra and Savarkar finally decided about the assassination of Wylie, Bhagat Singh wrote, "The two hugged each other. They were in tears. How invaluable and indelible that teardrop was. What would the cowardly people know about that emotion of those who aren't afraid of death, how would the cowards know that how holy, how revered, how high are the people who sacrifice their lives for the nation." ('Bhagat Singh aur unke sathiyon ke sampoorna uplabhda dastawej', page 166-168).

Noted historian YD Phadke says in his works on Savarkar published in Marathi ('Shodh Savarkrancha', Shrividya Prakashan, Pune) that Bhagat Singh got the English translation of Savarkar's work on the 1857 war of independence which was originally published as '1857 ka Swatantraya Samar'. The first edition of the English translation was published by another revolutionary Lala Hardayal. The third edition was published by Netaji Subhas Chandra Bose. The second edition was published by Bhagat Singh.

This book is considered to be one of the most influential works which not only challenged the British narrative of running down events in 1857 as a 'revolt' but also inspired scores of revolutionaries to fight against the British tyranny.

Bhagat Singh, has quoted in his "'Jail Diary' from Savarkar's another work on Hindu nationalism titled 'Hindupadpaadshahi' (The Hindu Empire). Bhagat Singh wrote while quoting 'Hindupadpaadshahi', "One can get rid of the political subjugation anytime but it is difficult to break away from the clutches of cultural slavery." He has used several other quotes from the same book.

After Bhagat Singh, Rajguru and Sukhdev were hanged, Savarkar penned a poem for them mourning their death and bowing to their valour and courage. The saffron flag on top of Savarkar's house at Ratnagiri was replaced by a black flag the day these three revolutionaries were martyred. Bhagwati Charan Vora and other fellow revolutionaries of Bhagat Singh have also mentioned at several places how Savarkar's revolutionary activities and his writings had a deep influence on all the revolutionaries including Bhagat Singh. These writings can be found in 'Bhagat Singh aur unke sathiyon ke sampoorna uplabhda dastawej' (Rahul Foundation, 2019) as mentioned earlier also.

❑

31

Gandhi and Savarkar: A Close Relationship

As one looks back at the legacy of Vinayak Damodar Savarkar (often known as Veer Savarkar), one of the most prominent ideologues of 'Hindutva' in the 20th Century, it is interesting to know that contrary to the common perception that both Gandhi and Savarkar were at loggerheads, both of them enjoyed such a good rapport that Gandhi referred to him as 'Bhai' (brother).

Mahatma Gandhi addressed Savarkar as 'Bhai' (brother) in a letter he wrote from Sevagram on 22 March 1945 ('Collected Works of Gandhi', E-Book, Publication Division, GOI, Volume 86, Page 86). Here is the text of the letter:

"BHAI SAVARKAR, I write this after reading the news of the death of your brother. I had done a little bit for his release and ever since I had been taking an interest in him. Where is the need to condole with you? We are ourselves in the jaws of death. I hope his family are all right. Yours, M. K. GANDHI."

In another letter ('Collected Works of Gandhi', Volume 38, page 138), Gandhi clearly mentioned, "I shall try to do whatever I can for political prisoners. It has never happened that I kept quiet out of fear. Even with regard to political prisoners, I would consider it improper to do anything for those who are in prison for crimes of murder. I shall not argue the point. I shall of course do my utmost for Bhai Vinayak Savarkar."

It all started with the efforts to take the Savarkar brothers out of the Cellular Jail in the Andamans. Gandhi was a vocal votary of getting both the Savarkar brothers released immediately. He was all praise for their sacrifice and spirit of nationalism.

Gandhi wrote in 'Young India' on 26 May, 1920 (Mahatma Gandhi: 'Collected Works', E-book, Publication Division, GOI, Volume 20, page 368-371) referring to a royal proclamation issued in December 1919 which had led to the release of many political prisoners except the Savarkar brothers:

"Thanks to the action of the Government of India and the Provincial Governments, many of those who were undergoing imprisonment at the time have received the benefit of the Royal clemency. But there are some notable "political offenders" who have not yet been discharged. Among these I count the Savarkar brothers. They are political offenders in the same sense as men, for instance, who have been discharged in the Punjab. And yet these two brothers have not received their liberty although five months have gone by after the publication of the Proclamation."

Defending VD Savarkar's elder brother, Gandhi wrote, "Mr Ganesh Damodar Savarkar, the elder of the two, was born in 1879, and received an ordinary education. He took a prominent part in the Swadeshi Movement at Nasik in 1908. He was sentenced to transportation for life with confiscation of property under Sections 121, 121A, 124A and 153A on the 9th day of June, 1909, and is now serving his sentence in the Andamans. He has therefore had eleven years of imprisonment. Section 121 is the famous section which was utilised during the Punjab trials and refers to 'waging war against the King'. The minimum penalty is transportation for life with forfeiture of property. 121A is a similar section. 124A relates to sedition. 153A relates to promotion of enmity between classes 'by words either spoken or written' or 'otherwise'. It is clear therefore that all the offences charged against Mr. Savarkar (senior) were of a public nature. He had done no violence. He was married, had two daughters who are dead, and his wife died about eighteen months ago."

About VD Savarkar, Gandhi said, "The other brother was born in 1884, and is better known for his career in London. His sensational attempt to escape the custody of the police and his jumping through a porthole in French waters, are still fresh in the public mind. He was educated at the Fergusson College, finished off in London and became a barrister. He is the author of the proscribed history of the Sepoy Revolt of 1857. He was tried in 1910, and received the same sentence as his brother on 24th December, 1910. He was charged also in 1911 with abetment of murder. No act of violence was proved against him either. He too is married, had a son in 1909. His wife is still alive."

"Now the only reason for still further restricting the liberty of the two brothers can be 'danger to public safety', for the Viceroy has been charged by His Majesty to exercise the Royal clemency to political offenders in the fullest manner which in his judgement is compatible with public safety. I hold therefore that unless there is absolute proof that the discharge of the two brothers who have already suffered long enough terms of imprisonment, who have lost considerably in body-weight and who have declared their political opinions, can be proved to be a danger to the State, the Viceroy is bound to give them their liberty. The obligation to discharge them, on the one condition of public safety being fulfilled, is, in the Viceroy's political capacity, just as imperative as it was for the Judges in their judicial capacity to impose on the two brothers the minimum penalty allowed by law. If they are to be kept under detention any longer, a full statement justifying it is due to the public."

"There is no question about the brothers being political offenders. And so far the public are aware, there is no danger to public safety. ...The public are entitled to know the precise grounds upon which the liberty of the brothers is being restrained."

In another letter to Shankerrao Deo dated 20 July 1937('Collected Works of Mahatma Gandhi': Volume 72, Page 50-51), Gandhi wrote, "About Shri Savarkar,

I did refuse to sign the memorial for, as I told those who came to me, it was wholly unnecessary as Shri Savarkar was bound to be released after the coming into force of the new Act, no matter who the Ministers were. And that is what has happened. The Savarkar brothers, at least, know that whatever the differences between us as to certain fundamentals, I could never contemplate with equanimity their incarceration. Perhaps, Dr Savarkar will bear me out when I say that I did whatever was in my power after my own way to secure their release. And the barrister (Veer Savarkar) will perhaps recall the pleasant relations that existed between us when we met for the first time in London and how, when nobody was forthcoming, I presided at the meeting that was held in his honour in London."

In a letter to MR Jayakar, dated, 25 February 1933, (Volume 59, page 384), Gandhi wrote, "I wonder if you were able to pass on my letter about the opening ceremony (of two temples in Ratnagiri) to Vinayakrao. He has certainly done very good social work in Ratnagiri."

When the Bihar Government had banned the annual session of the Hindu Mahasabha (Savarkar was the President of Hindu Mahasabha at that time) from being held between 1 December 1941 and 10 January 1942, Mahatma Gandhi came out openly defending the actions of Savarkar and Hindu Mahasabha by issuing a press statement from Bardoli on 27 December 1941(Volume 81, page-391-392). The statement read: "The action of the Bihar Government in banning the meeting of the Hindu Mahasabha has always appeared to me to be inexplicable. ... I see that Veer Savarkar had accommodated the Bihar authorities to the extent of postponing the session with a view to coming to an understanding. When all attempts at a settlement failed, civil resistance was the only remedy open to the suppressed Hindu Mahasabha. And I must confess it fills me with delight to find Veer Savarkar, Dr Moonje and other leaders being arrested in their attempt to assert the very primary and very fundamental right of holding an orderly meeting subject to all reasonable restrictions about the preservation of the public peace."

"I congratulate the leaders of the Sabha on their dignified and peaceful protest against the utterly arbitrary action of the Bihar Government. ...I hope that there will be only one end to this Bihar episode, viz., lifting of the ban on the Hindu Mahasabha and the men who are imprisoned today holding their session without let or hindrance."

Mahadev Desai gives an interesting account in his 'Weekly Letter' in Young India on 17 March 1927 about a meeting between Veer Savarkar and Gandhi at Ratnagiri that took place on 1 March 1927. Mahatma Gandhi had gone to enquire about the health of Savarkar who was not keeping well that that time. Desai wrote, "...Savarkar asked Gandhiji to clear his attitude about untouchability and shuddhi. Gandhiji cleared some of the misrepresentations and said: 'We cannot have long talk today, but you know my regard for you as a lover of truth and as one who would lay down his life for the sake of truth. Besides, our goal is ultimately one and I would like you to correspond with me as regards all points of difference between us. And more. I know that you cannot go out of Ratnagiri and I would not mind finding out two or three days to come and stay with you if necessary to discuss these things to our satisfaction." ('Collected Works of Gandhi': Volume 38, Page 176-180).

❑

32

Karl Marx's Grandson Admired Savarkar and Fought for him

Guess who defended Indian freedom fighter Vinayak Damodar Savarkar, who has been demonised by Marxists—historians and intelligentsia—consistently and persistently for his views on the ideology of Hindutva, in a case involving his daring escape to France. It was none other than Karl Marx's grandson!

Yes! It was Marx's grandson Jean-Laurent-Frederick Longuet (1876–1938), a French socialist, politician and journalist who not only stood to defend Savarkar in the International Court of Justice, The Hague but praised him for his bravery, patriotism and intellect.

Marx's grandson was born in London to Charles and Jenny Longuet, the family later moved to France. Jenny was Karl Marx's daughter. Jean Longuet worked as a journalist and got trained as a lawyer. He was also the founder and editor of the French newspaper Le Populaire and was a prominent socialist leader in France.

The Case

In a daring escape, Savarkar swam to the French sea shore at Marseilles on 8 July 1910, from 'Morea', a British merchant vessel, which was carrying him from Britain to India to start a trial against him for his revolutionary activities. He jumped into the sea through the porthole and swam to the sea shore at Marseilles.

While being pursued by British policemen from the vessel, he was captured by a French police officer, who returned him to the 'Morea', which sailed with Savarkar on board on the following day. Subsequently, France demanded the restitution of Savarkar on the ground that his delivery to the British officers on board the vessel was contrary to the rules of international law, and, upon Britain's refusal to comply, the dispute went for arbitration to a tribunal composed of the following members of the Permanent Court of Arbitration: August M F Beernaert of Belgium, Earl of Desart of England, Louis Renault of France, Gregors Gram of Norway and A F de Savornin Lohman of Holland. The case arguments began on 14 February 1911, and ended on 17 February 1911. The decision was delivered on 24 February 1911 in favour of Britain. Savarkar was sentenced to two life imprisonments in India later and sent to Cellular Jail at the Andamans, infamously known as 'Kaala Paani'.

Marx's grandson on Savarkar

It is a lesson for the dogmatic Left in India which opposes anything and everything related to the ideology of Hindutva, that Marx's grandson Longuet, who followed his grandfather's ideology, also found nothing wrong in being a 'Hindu nationalist'. Rather it seems he not only appreciated it, he was a great admirer of Savarkar and his beliefs.

Here is what he said in his appeal about Savarkar, "Mr. Savarkar took, from an early age, an active part in the agitation of the Hindu nationalist party, his two brothers, who were no less militant than he was, were sentenced, one to life imprisonment and one to several months' imprisonment for their participation in the Nationalist movement, are currently imprisoned. From the age of 22, a law student at the University of Bombay, he became the assistant of the famous Hindu, Tilak, and formed about the same time, in his native city, in Nasik, a national association known as the Mitra Mela, which like so many similar organizations, was engaged in an active propaganda throughout the Deccan, forming gymnastic societies, organizing meetings, where were read the biographies of the great national revolutionaries such as Shivaji and Ramdas and foreign ones such as Mazzini, whose memoir was fervently worshipped by Mr. Savarkar."

Longuet further added, "With his elder brother Ganesh, Sarvarkar was preaching everywhere with passion, the gospel of national independence, advocating armed uprising of his countrymen, according to the teachings of the founder of Italian independence. The rallying cry of the young nationalist was the cry which has since become famous throughout India 'Vande Mataram'. ('Hooray for the fatherland!'). In 1906, Mr. Vinayak Damodar Savarkar came to reside in England to complete his legal studies and be admitted to the bar in London, Gray's Inn section. He was 24 years old and filled with passion for revolutionary agitation in the colony of the great Hindu city, grouped around the India House, an institution created by a rich fellow. Mr. Krishnavarma, a former minister of one of the native states of Bengal, founded a chair at Oxford, dedicated to Herbert Spencer. Upon his arrival in the 'India House' Savarkar wrote the preface to a translation into Marathi of the 'Life of Mazzini.' Soon after, he began and finished a complete history of the 'War of Independence' in 1857, called by the British writers the 'Great Mutiny.' (This book, a real scientific value, was translated into English by several residents of India House and was published under the anonymous signature."

Most importantly Longuet said, "The last paragraph of his conclusion is characteristic of the thinking behind it: 'The Revolution of 1857', he wrote, 'is the test that showed how far India was in the path of unity, independence and popular force. Its failure was caused by men without energy, effeminate, selfish traitors who helped the enemy. But those who, bearing the sword, stained with their blood still warm, walked cheerfully to the fire and the battle to the death—not even a single voice rises to criticize these heroes! They were not fools, they were not reckless and they are not responsible for the defeat and that is why we cannot blame them. It is their call that has awakened Mother India from her deep sleep to march forward to overthrow slavery."

❑

33

Faiz Ahmad Faiz: A Fanatic who Pushed for Partition of India

Faiz Ahmad Faiz (1911–1984) was a renowned poet who is being projected as a Progressive thinker, writer/poet from Pakistan and very often in India also but contrary to this common perception, his writings reflect that he was he was a fanatic Muslim who pushed for partition of India. He was a fan of MA Jinnah. He worked closely with Muslim League leaders and post-independence continued his diatribe against India and Indians.

Faiz chose to become Editor-in-Chief of the Pakistan Times, a newspaper started by Muslim League leader Mian Iftikharuddin, a Punjabi politician who joined Muslim League after quitting the Indian National Congress (INC). Iftikharuddin's house and other properties were used for training National Guards of Muslim League who played havoc in the communal riots. Everyone knew this, including Faiz, but still he chose to remain with him.

Here are some more interesting details about

Mian Iftikharuddin on whose pay roll Faiz Ahmad Faiz chose to be till 1951 as Editor-in-Chief of the Pakistan Times.

Iftikharuddin was elected to the Punjab Provincial Assembly in 1946 as a Muslim League member. He was elected the first president of the Punjab Provincial Muslim League after the independence of Pakistan in 1947. He was also appointed as the Minister for rehabilitation of refugees in the government of Punjab in Pakistan. Iftikharuddin played an important role in fomenting trouble in Kashmir.

Interestingly, the newspaper started publication on 4 February 1947, around five months before Pakistan came into existence and Faiz was too happy to be its Editor-in-Chief. It was clear he believed in two-nation theory and that India should be divided on the basis of religion and yet he is called a PROGRESSIVE WRITER/POET!

Faiz's editorials: Loved Jinnah, Hated India

Let us take a look at some his editorials in the Pakistan Times which reveal his hatred towards India and his communal leanings.

Faiz on Partition (Editorial of the Pakistan Times dated 15 August 1947. The original title was: August 15)

"It is August 15 today. The dawn that brought this day into the world also restored to our people their long-lost freedom. Through many bleak decades of political serfdom, millions of us have waited and hoped for this dawn. It has arrived at last and yet, for us in the Punjab, it is not bright with laughter and buoyant with song. It is black with sorrow and red with blood. The heart does not lift to the great diction that has descended on us on this wonderful day and the reality of freedom, compared to the reality of the death and suffering around us, appears insubstantial and far away. While, in the West, the new edifice of Pakistan is emerging above its foundations, in the fire ravaged countryside of the East, the ancient homesteads of our less fortunate brothers are crumbling into ashes: while we are entering into our heritage, they are being turned out of theirs. It is a cruel tradition and our day of joyous thanksgiving is also the day of mourning. To enjoin and to practice a correct reaction to this day therefore, is difficult, and it is equally difficult to preach the pattern of collective and individual behaviour that should govern our actions today and hereafter. The difficulty, however, absolves no one of this duty to himself, to his people; and to the future of the great State that has today come into being. At a time of dire emergency, helplessness is as reprehensible as blind passion and to lose either courage or reason is criminal. Let us, therefore, try to put by our anger and our sorrow and look at things as they are. In Eastern Punjab, an undetermined number of Muslims villages have been destroyed, an indefinite number of Muslim men, women and children have been bestially butchered and the killing and destruction, as yet, show no sign of abatement. Our unfortunate country has witnessed other tragedies of a similar nature in recent times but a number of crucial factors which operated in Eastern Punjab, did not exist elsewhere. In the first place, the Provincial Governor who has against the will of the majority party in the Legislative, taken the responsibility for law and order upon him was fully aware of the menace that was developing. His administration was duly informed, both through their own resources and through repeated representations made to them by responsible public men, that one community was making extensive preparations for organised offence while the community marked out as the victim was being reduced to utter helplessness through forcible disarming. The answer of the Governor and his administration to these representations was to abet the arming of the belligerents and to enforce the disarming of their victims more vigorously than before. Secondly, while thousands of men were clapped into jail under various Safety Ordinance for merely suspected "dangerous thoughts." The Sikh leader who went about preaching fire and sword in every hamlet and town were allowed the maximum liberty of action and speech. All the stringent laws banning public meetings, provocative speeches, organisations for violence, etc. suddenly paled into invalidity at the remotest approach of hate-maddened communalists. Thirdly, even though the timing of the tragedy was known well in advance, the civil administration was allowed to go completely partisan precisely at the same juncture and to cap it all the entire Muslim police force stationed in Amritsar was collected and disarmed under false pretences. This last was the most treacherous act of all and its repercussions were frightful and immediate. It is impossible to believe, therefore, that the misfortunes of our brethren in the East were either a visitation of Fate or a calamitous upheaval of unforeseen communal frenzy. It appears to have been, on the other hand, cold-blooded premeditated murder and if the criminals are not made to appear the bar of justice, they will not escape the bar of history. Whatever the place assigned to Governor Jenkins in the annals of the Indian Civil Service, he will long be remembered in the history of the Punjab as either the most incompetent or the most unscrupulous occupant of the gubernatorial chair. How far his policy of setting the people of the Punjab at each other's throats has the tacit support or sanction of the British Government, we do not know, but if the British are still aiming to use the Sikhs as a permanent wedge between Pakistan and Hindustan they could not have found a better player to handle the cards. We regret to have to soil our pen on this day with this sordid tale but it has to be told and it has not yet concluded. Our brothers in the East are today the subjects of another State. We have no desire to cringe or whine before the new administration that has today taken over and we shall not enjoin this course on our brothers. We may not be able to render them any great material help, although we shall do the best we can, but we are fully confident that they will bear up bravely in the ordeal that confronts them and retain their self-respect and their solidarity, however hard these virtues might appear to be in the face of cold, mechanised destruction. Unlike Acharya Kripalani we shall not talk of the hostages of the other community that are among us, as one innocent life is no repayment for another, and one burnt out homestead does not regain its inhabited contentment, if we burn out another. Revenge and retaliation may appear to some as normal and human, frenzy and passion may be mistaken for love and courage. We have to realize, however, that the only real support that we can render to our people outside Pakistan is to make Pakistan so strong and so powerful that all our neighbours are forced to territories. We cannot even set about this task if we encourage lawlessness and disorder and violence in our midst, whatever the end in view. We have no moment to fritter away in idle destruction, not a sinew, nor a muscle to spare for any task except the urgent tasks of constructing and fortifying the State we have won, after countless years of suffering and privation. Our present sorrow is but a passing phase and must not be allowed to damage our national heritage that is permanent and enduring. Let us enter into our heritage, devoutly and thankfully, even though the steps are stained with blood and the threshold washed in tears."

Faiz on Jinnah (Editorial of the Pakistan Times dated 27 Dec 1947. The original title was: HOMAGE)

"As we write, the Muslims of India and Pakistan are celebrating the birthday of the Quaid-i-Azam. As the man who has propelled, guided and controlled the national policies of nearly hundred million human souls, the man who has been responsible for the birth of a major State and the liberation of a major nation from economic and political bondage, the Quaid-i-Azam has already passed into history. With the establishment of Pakistan the mandate entrusted to him by his people may be considered to have been fulfilled and his historical role as the architect of our national State may be said to have reached its glorious consummation. The attainment of this objective demanded a steadiness of vision, fixity of purpose, an amount of unflagging devotion and courage that are rarely found among a people, broken and debased by enslavement and exploitation. The history of nations however is continuum like time, and the culmination of one struggle merely means the commencement of another. The mission of our national leaders, therefore, is far from complete and the national objective we have formally attained still awaits its material content. The future of Indian Muslims who have done as much and suffered far more for Pakistan than we the Muslims of Pakistan have, is still uncertain, and the State of Pakistan has still to require the constitutional flesh and bone. Both these problems are of as great an importance to us as the achievement of Pakistan itself and their satisfactory solution will require an equal amount of vision, determination and courage. There are already many among us, men of small minds and smaller vision, who think that the future of our brothers beyond the border need not enter our national calculations and now that we have got Pakistan, the future of non-Pakistanis is none of our business. The happenings in East Pakistan have utterly negated our thesis and proved that our kinsmen in the neighbouring Dominion are very much our business that we have got to take them into calculation while formulating our national policies. We have got to ensure that these policies do not in any way adversely affect the national existence of our co-religionists in the other land, through injudiciousness or lack of imagination. Similarly, we have to ensure that both the constitutional structure and the governmental practice of the Pakistani State conform to the ideals that we put before ourselves when we embarked on our national struggle. We have not yet had a glimpse of the Pakistan of our dreams, for we are still besieged by all the ills that have plagued us in the past and the common man has yet to taste the contentment, physical and spiritual, of a free and prosperous existence. The helmsmen of the nation, therefore, of whom the Quaid-i-Azam is the greatest and the most indefatigable, have far from reached the end of their labours and the future of the nation depends as much on their sagacity today as it has dependent on their industry and devotion in the past."

Faiz on Baluchistan:

(Faiz's editorial of the Pakistan Times dated 29 June 1947. Original title was: Baluchistan)

"On June, 30th the representatives of Baluchistan consisting of the Shahi Jirga (excluding the Kalat State nominees) and non-official members of the Quetta Municipality, will be called upon to record their vote in favour of joining either of the Constituent Assemblies. From all indications, public opinion in that Province is overwhelmingly in favour of entering the Pakistan Constituent Assembly. Only isolated voices are heard (as one was the other day), Baluchistan should negotiate with the Congress as well as the League, and side with that body which offers the most advantageous terms. Apart from the fact that any hesitation to choose between Muslim India and Hindu India reflects ill on the national consciousness of those who advocated this petty bargaining, did they pause to think that the Congress could now offer them nothing. The Congress no longer finds it practical politics to take a Muslim Province directly under its wing. It now knows, to its cost, that the game is not worthwhile; and instead of figuring as a directly interested party in the coming referendums, it encourages its stooges to discard their old labels and assume newer and ostensibly more appealing ones. The NWFP has to offer Baluchistan an object lesson. Having despaired of drawing the Frontier Province into its fold, the Congress has signalised its defeat by boycotting the referendum, under pretexts which do not invest its necessity with even a semblance of virtue. If Khan Abdul Ghaffar has broken away from the Congress on the ground that by accepting Dominion State it has betrayed its creed we would have credited him with honesty and consistent principles. His leadership was Congress-sustained and now stands exhausted of its entire dynamics. The Frontier referendum is expected to be walk-over for the League, and neutralise this plainest that other objectives are sought, and abstention from the referendum is prescribed. The example of the Frontier Khanate should not be lost upon Congress henchmen, if there be any, in Baluchistan. It is not only geography, but religion and ideology as well, that render Baluchistan's kinship with Pakistan, all the closer. It is hoped that the Baluch Province will enthusiastically respond to the call of the great leader, who has served it and the rest of Muslim India, for ten years, with a wholehearted devotion, singleness of purpose and unrivalled sagacity. There will be efforts, some of them may be determined and even ingenious to disrupt Muslim unity in Baluchistan; but it is for the Baluchis to present a solid, invincible form against all such machinations. The Muslims of Sylhet will also be faced with a similar situation and it goes without saying that they will cast their vote for Muslim solidarity."

(Source: The above editorials have been sourced from http://www.faizcentenary.org/articles_by_faiz.htm.)

❑

34

1956 Niyogi Committee and Meenakshipuram 1981: Defining Moments of Debate on Religious Conversions

The debate on 'religious conversions' in India continues to get reignited every now and then cases of conversion of Hindus to Islam or Christianity coming to light quite frequently.

There has been an attempt to build a perception that the 'religious conversions' issue has been used by Hindu outfits in the country to consolidate Hindu votes, and it is being raked up whenever polls are around.

However, it is a fact that the issue of religious conversions is not related to electoral politics as much as many may want it to be. There are two crucial and defining movements in the journey this debate has witnessed since Independence, and both times it had nothing to do with electoral politics.

The first defining moment was the Niyogi

Committee Report On Christian Missionary Activities in 1956 when the Bharatiya Jana Sangh (BJS), the forerunner of the present-day Bharatiya Janata Party (BJP), was a very junior player in national politics. The second crucial moment was the conversion of a number Scheduled Caste Hindus to Islam in Meenakshipuram (Tamil Nadu) in 1981.

Niyogi committee report

The Niyogi committee was set up by the Congress government in Madhya Pradesh after several complaints of conversion of tribal Hindus to Christianity came up.

A look at the committee's key findings shows how serious the issue of religious conversions was even at that time. "On consideration of the material" before it, the report arrived at the following "conclusions of fact":

1. Since the Constitution of India came into force there has been an appreciable increase in the American personnel of the Missionary organisations operating in India. This increase is obviously due to the deliberate policy of the International Missionary Council to send evangelistic teams to areas of special opportunities opened to the Gospel by the Constitutional provision of religious freedom in some of the newly independent nations, equipped with new resources for mass evangelism through the press, film, radio and

television (Pages 27 and 31 of 'The Missionary Obligation of the Church', 1952).

2. Enormous sums of foreign money flow into the country for Missionary work, comprising educational, medical and evangelist activities. It was out of such funds received from abroad that in Surguja the Lutherans and other proselytizing agencies were able to secure nearly 4,000 converts.

3. Conversions are mostly brought about by undue influence, misrepresentation, etc., or in other words not by conviction but by various inducements offered for proselytization in various forms. Educational facilities such as free gifts of books and education are offered to secure the conversion of minors in the primary and secondary schools under the control of the Missions. Moneylending is one of the various forms adopted as a mild form of pressure to induce proselytization. This is found very prominently in the case of Roman Catholic Missions operating in the hill tracts of Surguja, Raigarh, Mandla, etc. Cases where coercion was reported to have been used are generally of those converts who wish other members of the family to join their Christian parents or to secure girls in marriage.

4. Missions are in some places used to serve extra religious ends. In spite of assurances given by foreign and national Missionaries to authorities, instances of indirect political

activities were brought to the notice of the Committee.

5. As conversion muddles the converts' sense of unity and solidarity with his society, there is a danger of his loyalty to his country and State being undermined.
6. A vile propaganda against the religion of the majority community is being systematically and deliberately carried on so as to create an apprehension of breach of public peace.
7. Evangelization in India appears to be a part of the uniform world policy to revive Christendom for re-establishing Western supremacy and is not prompted by spiritual motives. The objective is apparently to create Christian minority pockets with a view to disrupt the solidarity of the non-Christian societies, and the mass conversion of a considerable section of Adivasis with this ulterior motive is fraught with danger to the security of the State.
8. Schools, hospitals and orphanages are used as a means to facilitate proselytization.
9. Tribals and Harijans are the special targets of aggressive evangelization for the reason that there is no adequate provision of hospitals, schools, orphanages and other social welfare services in the scheduled or specified areas.
10. The Government of Madhya Pradesh have throughout followed a policy of absolute

> neutrality and non-interference in matters concerning religion and allegations of discrimination against Christians and harassment of them by Government officials have not been established. Such allegations have been part of the old established policy of the Missions to overawe local authority and to carry on propaganda in foreign countries.

The outcome of this report in the socio-cultural arena was significant. It was one of the key triggers for the formation of Vishva Hindu Parishad and expansion of the work of Vanvasi Kalyan Ashram, which has ever since worked across India to check conversions. Both these outfits were set up by the volunteers of Rashtriya Swayamsevak Sangh.

What happened after Meenakshipuram conversions

The Meenakshipuram incident led to a furore in the country with the RSS taking up the issue in a big way.

The VHP took the lead and an organisation by the name of Virat Hindu Samaj was set up, which organised a 'Virat Hindu Sammelan' in Delhi and it estimated to have been attended by five lakh people.

Such conferences were organised all over the country at state and district levels. The issue was also raised in Parliament.

One of the offshoots of this debate has been the issue of 'love jihad'.

However, it is clear that the debate on religious conversions in India has been continuing for the last seven decades and would continue to do so, until these conversions by force or fraud are checked. Thus, it isn't about merely garnering some additional votes by consolidation of Hindu votes—the debate is much bigger and much larger.

❑

35

How RSS inspired Mausi Kelkar to build Rashtra Sevika Samiti

The Rashtriya Swayamsevak Sangh (RSS), arguably the largest voluntary organisation in the world, has often been targeted by its detractors on the issue of its worldview about women.

But contrary to the stereotypes nurtured by its critics since its inception, the RSS is not a patriarchal organisation. In 1936, RSS founder Dr. KB Hedgewar inspired educationist Lakshmi Bai Kelkar, who was a young widow, with its ideology, leading to the formation of an all-women organisation called the Rashtra Sevika Samiti.

In 'The RSS Roadmaps for 21st Century' (Rupa Publications, 2019), senior RSS pracharak Sunil Ambekar wrote, "The fact that during an age of rampant social conservatism riddled with normative assumptions, Doctorji (Hedgewar) was a firm believer in the intellectual capabilities of women, shows his open-mindedness."

He added, "At that time, to hold several rounds

of conversations with a widowed woman about starting a parallel women-only organisation was out of the ordinary. Doctorji explained the Sangh's beliefs, methods, objectives and other technical details to Mausi Kelkar (Lakshmi Bai Kelkar). As a result Sevika Samiti was formed after adopting the form and content of the Sangh for women."

Today, the Samiti has its own full-time workers, daily shakhas and holds various activities across two dozen countries around the world. While the Samiti's structure is fairly similar to the RSS, its activities are different. Since its formation, it has developed its own methodology to engage with women.

Just as the RSS has full-time workers known as pracharaks, the Samiti also has pracharikas. There are short-time workers too, who work for the Samiti for a period of two years.

The Samiti also has a uniform and holds training camps for its cadres—first-year, second-year and third-year. The duration of each camp is around 15 days, which are held annually in May-June.

According to the Samiti's records, over 10,000 women attend these camps across the country annually. The first such camp was held in 1939. During the Samiti's 80th year celebrations in 2016, its training camp was attended by 3,000 sevikas (volunteers).

The work of the Nagpur-headquartered organisation has reached every sub-division in the country, with around 5,000 shakhas and 900 welfare projects.

According to its documents, the Samiti focuses on Hindu women's role in the society as leaders and agents of positive social reform, and teaches them three ideals: matrutva (universal motherhood), kartrutva (efficiency and social activism) and netrutva (leadership).

Samiti's journey

The growth of Rashtra Sevika Samiti is synonymous with the journey of its founder Lakshmi Bai Kelkar, who was born on 6 July 1905, and is known by her followers as 'Mausiji'.

Widowed at the age of 27, when she was the mother of a young girl, Kelkar often worried about where to educate her daughter. She was so committed to this cause that she decided to set up a school for educating girls. Named Kesarimal Kanya Vidyalaya, the school is still functional.

She then met RSS founder Dr. KB Hedgewar, who had founded the Sangh in 1925, and held several rounds of discussions with him. Following this, she started the organisation and dedicated herself to build a nationwide organisational network.

As the first head of the organisation, she was called Pramukh Sanchalika. She retained the title until her death in 1978. Currently, Shanta Kumari—a postgraduate in mathematics with an M.Ed degree—holds the title. She worked as a teacher in Bharatiya Vidya Bhawan in Bengaluru before taking voluntary retirement in 1995 to devote full time for the organisational work.

According to a senior functionary of the Samiti who did not wish to be named, the organisation is now focusing on expanding its base in adolescents, especially college students. A separate wing, 'Taruni Vibhag', has been set up to engage with the younger girls and women. The results have been quite encouraging, said the Samiti functionary. "We foresee a rapid expansion in our activities amongst adolescents and the youth in days to come," she added.

❑❑❑